DEAD OR ALIVE

John Creasey Master crime fiction writer John Creasey's 562 titles have sold more than 80 million copies in over 25 languages. After enduring 743 rejection slips, the young Creasey's career was kickstarted by winning a newspaper writing competition. He went on to collect multiple honours from The Mystery Writers of America including the Edgar Award for best novel in 1962 and the coveted title of Grand Master in 1969. Creasey's prolific output included 11 different series including Roger West, the Toff, the Baron, Patrick Dawlish, Gideon, Dr Palfrey, and Department Z, published both under his own name and 10 other pseudonyms.

Creasey was born in Surrey in 1908 and, when not travelling extensively, lived between Bournemouth and Salisbury for most of his life. He died in England in 1973.

The Department Z Series

DEAD OR ALIVE

Department Z

JOHN CREASEY

ipso books

This edition published in 2017 by Ipso Books

First published in 1951 in Great Britain by Evans Brothers Ltd.

Ipso Books is a division of Peters Fraser + Dunlop Ltd

Drury House, 34–43 Russell Street, London WC2B 5HA

Chapter 1
The Snatch

The smiling young man sitting on the park bench spoke in a low-pitched, friendly voice.

"You can choose for yourself, Professor, but they're my orders—to take you dead or alive. You can shout for help and try to run, and either way you'll be killed. Much better be sensible, and come with me."

Professor Julian Conway glanced at a young woman passing within two yards of the bench. She was hurrying, young and eager, and with glistening eyes. She had a figure which he could hardly fail to notice, because it was hot and she wore only a light cotton dress. Her legs were bare, she wore sandals, and the red varnish on the toe-nails looked like blood. She had probably never thought seriously about death, or if it came to that, about life; she just lived.

Suddenly, she waved, and her pace quickened. From some way off, a beaming youth hurried towards her. About them were the trees and shrubs of St. James's Park, not far away was the lake with its pretty ducks and wild-fowl.

Only the young hurried. Within earshot were several dozen people; within sight, many more.

The Professor turned to the smiling young man, who wore a light-grey flannel suit, looked cool and immaculate, and whose handsome face with its crown of dark, sleek hair drew the glances of most of the girls who passed.

"And if you kill me, what will happen to you?" he asked mildly.

"I'll take my chance, Professor, you needn't worry about me—you've enough to worry about as it is. Be sensible—it doesn't have to be the hard way."

"Who employs you?" asked the Professor.

It was a simple question; he was known to be a man of simple ways; and was also known to be a genius. He didn't look it. His greying hair was a little long, he had weak eyes helped by thick-lensed glasses, behind which he blinked frequently. His long face, with the sunken cheeks, was pale; and he needed a shave. He wore a shabby, dark-grey suit, which made him too warm, and his forehead and upper lip glistened with tiny beads of sweat. His expression was gentle, and his lips suggested kindliness; nothing about him indicated that he was a repository of many closely guarded secrets.

"You needn't worry about my employer," said the handsome young man, who was no more than thirty. "Just come along with me. You'll be well looked after, provided you're helpful no one will hurt you; you'll have a modern laboratory and everything you could wish. That's a promise."

"How kind of you," Professor Conway smiled gently.

"You'll be told, but not by me. There's money in it, too— much more than you get out of the Government."

The Professor fanned himself with a tattered copy of that day's *Times*.

"I've never been very interested in money."

"I know all about you," said the young man. "More than you know yourself, probably. You're not interested in hard cash, but you have to live. We'd look after your daughter.

If you come with me, you needn't worry about anything or anyone, but if you make difficulties——" He shrugged, and couldn't have smiled more broadly had he been talking to a child. "Well, you can never tell, can you? Nice girl, Alice."

"Oh, yes," agreed the Professor enthusiastically, "she is charming! Did you notice the girl who passed just now, hurrying to her sweetheart? She reminded me of Alice—the same eagerness, the same youthfulness. Alice is older, of course—why, she must be twenty-five. How time flies!"

"It's flying too fast now, and I mustn't stay much longer. Coming?"

The Professor blinked.

"I haven't yet decided. Be patient, young man—you young people are always in too much of a hurry. If I refuse, you will kill me, you say?"

"Just like that."

"How?"

"That's my secret."

"I was reading a book the other day," said the Professor mildly, "and something rather like this happened. The author made it clear that bluff——"

The pleasant voice hardened. "I'm not bluffing."

"How can I be sure?" asked the Professor. "This was a true-life book, everything in it really happened—it was fascinating. I sat back when I'd finished, and asked myself how I should behave if I were suddenly threatened. I thought I should be horribly frightened, but do you know, young man, I don't feel the least bit nervous."

"You needn't, if you come with me."

"You repeat yourself so much," said the Professor reprovingly. "On the other hand, you must be a man of considerable courage. You are probably much more nervous than I, in spite of your calm manner. If I refuse, you will have to kill me and take your chance at escaping. If you failed, you would be hanged by the neck until you were dead—what an ugly phrase, isn't the law brutal in some ways? I am not in favour of hanging."

"I shouldn't be hanged. I'd kill myself."

"Really! Tell me, are you doing this for money?"

"You're talking too much."

The harsh note in the young man's voice was more pronounced. He didn't look away from the Professor, who studied his dark, brown eyes, the thin black eyebrows and moustache.

"I insist on knowing—are you taking this risk for money or for an ideal?"

"Supposing we say both? And supposing we say you've two minutes left?"

The people walking to and fro kept glancing at them, for they made an ill-assorted couple. It was early evening, and more people were passing now, mostly in one direction—away from the West End towards Buckingham Palace and beyond. Among them was a policeman, walking with ponderous tread, glancing about him, red-faced and sticky hot in his dark-blue serge. His helmet towered above his head, worn at exactly the proper angle. He was less than twenty yards away.

The young man's right hand dropped to his pocket. The Professor saw the movement, but didn't change his expression. The constable plodded past, and the young man gradually relaxed and wiped his forehead with his left hand.

"Yes, you are much more frightened than I," said the Professor. "I wish I had the courage to defy you."

"You wouldn't last ten seconds."

"I'm beginning to believe you," said the Professor. "If you were bluffing, I don't think you would be so much on edge. Where have we to go?"

"Just come with me."

"May I send a message to my daughter?"

"I'll see to that."

"What will you tell her?"

"That you've gone away on important secret business—again. It won't surprise her, as you've done it before."

"You aren't very free with your information, are you?" complained the Professor.

He stood up.

That had a surprising effect, for he was well over six feet tall, and very thin. His trousers were too short, and showed gay-coloured socks, which clashed horridly with his dark suit. The sleeves of the coat were also short, yet the coat seemed a little too big for him. His stiff white collar was at least two sizes too large, and he had a prominent Adam's apple.

The handsome young man was tall, but not so tall as the Professor.

"No tricks," he said. "We're going straight on."

He ranged himself by the Professor's side, and they walked briskly towards St. James's Palace and then turned right, towards the Admiralty Arch and Trafalgar Square.

Every now and again the young man glanced round, as if he were nervous of being followed, but he made no comment. The Professor appeared to take an amiable interest in everything about him. He showed intense pleasure at the fluttering scurry of the pigeons in Trafalgar Square, the crowd of people gathered about them, the children tossing dried peas and crumbs, the photographers posing the children with birds on their arms and heads. In spite of the heat, everything here was brisk. The fountains were working at full pressure, the hissing white spray and the water in the pools giving an illusion of coolness.

They passed these and then the massive structure of St. Martin-in-the-Fields. Still the young man kept glancing behind him, and kept his right hand in his pocket, his left on the Professor's arm.

They took a side street.

As they approached a sleek-looking black car the engine started up. The couple reached this car, and the young man said:

"In you get."

"What a luxurious automobile," said the Professor. He got in, sank back on the seat, and gently wiped his forehead.

The car moved off.

CHAPTER 2
THE TRICK

Peter Ross lifted his pink gin.

"To you, beautiful," he said, "and may your shadow ever grow less."

He sipped.

Mae Harrison looked at him over the top of her glass, a trick which showed off the beauty of her grey-green eyes with their golden flecks. She had true beauty spoiled only by her own awareness of it and the illusion that she was irresistible. Her golden hair was cut short and curled round her head like a feather cap; she was perfectly made-up. She wore a black strapless gown, and her mink wrap was hanging over the back of her chair, only partly because it was warm in the Dive. Her shoulders and arms were flawless.

"Darling," she cooed, "if anyone else had said that, I should have thought he meant that I was getting fat."

"Never!"

"Darling, you aren't cooling off me, are you?"

"I've never been so hot."

"Darling," said Mae, "I'm not sure that I believe you. But I'm not going to let you go easily."

"Talons well in," murmured Ross. "Your supreme virtue is brutal frankness, precious. Didn't I buy you that be-ootiful ring?"

The engagement ring scintillated, the brightest thing in the little niche of brightness in London's drab night.

Mae glanced at it, spreading out her fingers. Fate had been too kind to her; she was beautiful in every detail, her fingers were long, her hands slender and delicately white, and she did not make the mistake of tipping her nails with blood-red varnish.

"With that ring you bound us together, precious."

"Nothing tighter than gold! What makes you think I'm beginning to regret it?"

"Just you, darling."

"I haven't altered," declared Ross, and straightened up to peer at himself in a nearby mirror. About them were dozens of other people, mostly young, several more mirrors, a bar with many coloured bottles behind it, a Negro bartender, named Sam, because the Dive had to be 'different'. The little tables were crowded, and the inevitable hum of conversation was broken by bursts of laughter and an occasional "Yes, *sah*" from Sam. "Look at me—handsome as ever, no grey hairs, tie in the right place."

He touched the bow and pulled down his jacket. His evening clothes were from Savile Row, he was lean, lithe, of medium height—but no one could ever call him handsome, because many years ago someone had broken his nose.

"You look the same and talk the same," said Mae. "But you don't act the same."

"Now, precious…"

"*Da*rling," cooed Mae, "I know it's probably a mistake and I might grow out of it, but I love you."

"Easy on the syrup," said Ross, and glanced about him with exaggerated uneasiness. "Someone might hear you, we must keep that kind of thing to ourselves. When we're all nice and cosy, and…"

"That's just it."

"Eh?"

"Darling, you're not deaf, and you know what I mean. That's just the trouble. It's ten days since we spent a full evening together. I don't want part of you, I want every minute, not an odd hour and a drink and a sudden disappearance and apologies and excuses anyone could see through. You don't really think I'm dumb, do you?"

"Not in a thousand years! But work…"

"I don't believe you. It's not work."

"Honest toil," said Ross, and leaned forward and patted her hand. "It will come to an end, and…"

"Prove it's work," she challenged.

Ross looked pained.

"No trust? What a foundation for unhappy marriage! Sorry, sweet." His voice was firmer. "It's hush-hush, you know that as well as I do. I'm not simply a pilot, I have to be in at conferences and this and that, and the Powers That Be don't consider aching hearts and the fact that I'd rather be with you than with them. Don't let's spoil the evening."

"I've never known any other pilot who had to disappear so often as you do."

"But did you ever know another man like me?"

"Not quite like you," admitted Mae. "The others were always ready to bow and scrape, that was one of the things that made me fall for you. Peter…"

"Another?" He took her empty glass.

"Don't get up," ordered Mae firmly, and leaned forward and grasped his wrist. "Peter, I'm in earnest. I'm not seeing

9

you often enough, and I don't believe all your excuses. I want to know when we can start living normally again."

"These experimental jobs…"

"There are other pilots."

"Not for this job, I've been on it too long."

"And that makes you indispensable, does it? What will happen if the plane blows up in mid-air or you crash?"

"Need we be grisly?"

"I'm just being realistic. It's bad enough to have that fear hanging over my head. I'm frightened half the time you're away from me, in case…"

"So you take my word for it that I fly?" Ross grinned. "Forget it, sweet, and have another. Then…"

"I won't forget it. If anything were to happen to you, they'd have to find another pilot, so there's bound to be someone else who can fly the aeroplane and knows as much as you do about this secret one. You see, darling, I *can* add two and two together. If you were to resign, the other man would take your place, your pride might be hurt a little, but I'd make up for that."

Ross leaned back in his chair and watched her levelly. She was undoubtedly the most beautiful woman among many beauties here. Her face and figure were things to dream about, and she was dressed by Dior. He knew her faults, and wasn't worried by them. It was not only her beauty and melting softness which had made him fall in love, there was a quality in Mae which others couldn't see; and some said didn't exist.

"Isn't this dangerous ground, Mae?"

"I'm serious."

"Forcing the issue—choose between me and your work, all feminine and coy."

"Not coy, darling, and your work is suspect."

Ross said: "The job should be through in a month, but might take longer. After that, we'll get married and..."

"Before that, precious."

Ross took her hand again. His eyes were hazel brown, could twinkle and be merry and could be deadly serious; and they were serious then. They watched each other intently, oblivious of everyone else in the room, of everything but themselves. Ross's hand was lean and brown, and there was great strength in it.

"Don't force this any further, Mae."

"I must, Peter. Oh, I don't seriously think there's another woman, but I can't share you with this work. I get fiendishly jealous, and it isn't good for me and can't be good for you." She drew in her breath softly. "Give it up, Peter."

"And regret it all my life? No."

"I tell you I'm in deadly earnest."

"That goes for me, too."

Mae said: "I'll stop you, somehow."

"I shouldn't, darling, just accept the fact that there's part of me you can't have—but it's not much. Pink gin again?"

"Peter, will you drop this job?"

"No."

Mae shrugged and smiled, and her beauty was intense enough to hurt. She slid the engagement ring from her finger and pushed it across the shiny surface of the table. It touched a spot of liquid, and a wet line was made on the polish. The diamond scintillated as if it were aflame. Ross looked into Mae's eyes, not at the ring, and his lips were set, but his heart was thumping and he knew what it was to feel despair.

"You can offer it again, when you've dropped the job," said Mae. "I *might* take it back. Don't wait too long."

She stood up, smiled at him radiantly, picked up her wrap and draped it round her lovely shoulders. He was still getting to his feet when she reached the door. She didn't look round again, but a dozen people glanced at Ross, and he covered the diamond swiftly with his hand. He sat back in his chair, forcing himself not to rush after her.

He'd been sitting there for five minutes, glancing at the door, trying to pretend that he was expecting Mae back, when a waiter sidled across to him.

"Telephone, Mr. Ross."

"Oh. Thanks."

Ross stood up, paid for the drinks, and went out, nodding to ebony-faced Sam and his flash of white teeth, smiling at two or three acquaintances; he felt the interest, knew that the quarrel had been noticed and would become common gossip overnight.

The telephone was in a corner, just outside the bar. He picked it up.

"Peter Ross here."

"Come at once, will you?" said a man whose voice was as familiar as Mae's—and a man whom he had to obey.

Ross knew that Mae was serious, yet fought against believing it. He watched the door of the ladies' room, actually waited for two or three minutes before he went farther on to the landing and up the narrow, carpeted stairs which led from the Dive. The commissionaire was on duty in the narrow entrance hall; he saluted smartly, and appeared to be staring with more than his usual interest.

"Taxi, sir?"

"No, thanks. Good night." Ross walked into the street, which was tucked away between Oxford Street and Grosvenor Square. It was a calm, cool night, and the freshness was welcome after the warmth of the bar.

They'd come in Mae's car; so she'd driven off, or the commissionaire wouldn't have offered to get a taxi. Yet Ross glanced towards the spot where he had parked the gleaming Lagonda. He walked past the dozen other cars nearby, brisk and purposeful, set-faced. In Grosvenor Square a taxi drew near with its lighted sign on.

"Taxi!" Ross waved, and the cab pulled up. "Whitehall—just past the Cenotaph, Parliament Street side."

He sank back, and still watched the passing cars and the people, saw a Lagonda and peered at it; a man was at the wheel next to a woman much older than Mae. He lit a cigarette, leaned back and closed his eyes.

A little more than ten minutes later he paid the taxi off and stood near the Cenotaph's simplicity, glancing up and down—no longer looking for Mae, but making sure that he hadn't been followed. Then he walked to a narrow street and paused again, to make sure no one took any interest in him. At last he approached a narrow door in the side of one of the big Ministry buildings—a door so small and inconspicuous that many people who passed it daily hardly knew it was there; strangers seldom noticed it. There was a pale light, a flight of stone steps and a handrail. He didn't go up immediately, but returned to the door and, without showing himself, glanced in each direction. For the first time he felt that he could be sure that he hadn't been followed.

He went up four short flights of stairs, and stopped opposite a blank wall. He slid his fingers beneath the rail, and found what seemed to be a tiny crack in the wood. He pressed his finger-nail into this crack, and after a short pause, the 'wall' opened, showing a sliding-door, a tiny cubicle, and, through a second door, a large room.

A big man stood in front of him.

"Hallo, Bill," said Ross.

"Hallo, Peter. You were quick."

Ross entered the big room, and was conscious of the thoughtful gaze of the big man, and also of another, smaller man who sat in an easy chair in front of a small coal fire. This nearer end of the room was like that of one in any flat. There was a small table, a bookshelf, an open fireplace with many oddments on it, some photographs, two easy chairs, and, by the side of the oak fender, a pair of leather slippers. In the corner was a large cupboard, the door open; the end of a piece of string hung down. This section of the room was homely and pleasant, in sharp contrast to the other, larger part, where there were cold, green-metal desks, with several telephones on each, a typewriter on one, a green metal filing-cabinet, a dictaphone.

The door slid to behind Ross, as silently as it had opened. He went to the fire and, looking at the smaller man, spread out his hands.

"Hallo, Gordon. Still at it?"

Gordon Craigie didn't answer.

"We just wanted a cosy little chat with you," said the big man.

The word 'cosy' jarred, and Ross turned sharply. The big man was smiling amiably. He had a genially ugly face, and was running to fat. His waistcoat was rumpled and spread with tobacco ash. He needed a hair-cut, and that emphasised the grey sides of his head, although at first glance his hair seemed dark.

"Take a pew."

"Thanks," said Ross, and sat down. "Here we are again, then, the great Gordon Craigie and his brilliant assistant, William Loftus, looking as mysterious as ever. Don't you two ever get tired of play-acting?"

"Play-acting?" murmured Loftus.

"The secret door, sliding-panels, green and red lights, all the fun of the fair," said Ross, and forced a laugh.

"Gordon's fond of the trappings," said Loftus. "I've protested myself, but he has the final answer—they work. Gives the Department a nice feeling of mystery and intrigue, too, which puts us in the right mood. I hope."

"Who am I to argue?" asked Ross.

"That's right." Loftus continued to smile.

Silence fell; Ross found it awkward, and hadn't found that in this room before. It was rather like the quiet at the Dive, before he'd left. He told himself that it was his imagination, took out a cigarette and stretched his legs, stifled a yawn, and said:

"What's it tonight?"

"Getting tired of it, Peter?" asked Gordon Craigie, almost lazily.

"My dear chap! What an idea!"

Loftus said: "Gordon's a wise old bird, Peter. Why not tell him your troubles?"

Craigie looked a man in his early sixties; he was actually fifty-two. He had a long face, thin cheeks, a lantern jaw and deep ridges at the sides of his mouth, from which a meerschaum drooped. He wore an old smoking-jacket, his thin grey hair was standing on end at the back, his grey eyes looked tired. But he smiled as Ross looked at him sharply— and reminded Ross exactly of a wise old bird.

"Now what's this?" Ross asked.

Craigie said: "Let's have a drink, Bill." Loftus moved to the corner cupboard and busied himself with bottles and glasses. "Peter, you know the kind of job we're on, and you know you're good. Probably the best man we have working today, although you haven't been with us long. I don't want to spend a lot of time back-slapping, but we need good men, and this job may need a little bit extra from everyone. It needs single-mindedness, too—everything you have."

Loftus thrust a whisky and soda into Ross's hand.

"Thanks. Meaning what?"

"What was the trouble between you and Mae tonight?"

Ross started, and a little of the whisky spilled on his finger. He put the glass down steadily and moistened his lips. He ought to have suspected this, from the manner of the two men. He drew too hard at his cigarette, and was uncomfortably aware of Craigie's faint smile and the set stare from Loftus.

"Well, well," he said, "so it's really true. Department Z has eyes everywhere. I was fool enough to think that you trusted me."

"Ass," said Loftus.

"I'm not so sure..."

"Idiot," said Loftus, and gulped down half his drink.

Craigie chuckled.

"Both right, and you knew it, Peter. We can't afford to have anyone running around without being watched, if you were to run into a bus we'd need to know pretty quickly. You might even get a knife in your ribs or a bullet in your chest—and if we have someone watching, it's even possible that the knife or the bullet wouldn't get home. You can scoff at the trappings, but you can't dispense with them in the Service. Don't get some silly notion that we're halfhearted about trusting you—there isn't anything we wouldn't trust you with, normally."

"Normally," Ross echoed.

"You had a quarrel of some kind with Mae tonight, and it might have been no more than a tiff, but it could be sufficient to unsettle you. That might justify us in keeping you off a special job, mightn't it? And if it happened when you were on a job and you started thinking of two things at once, it would make the difference between living and dying."

He talked as if this were the most normal subject in the world.

Ross tossed his drink down.

"Well, where do we go from here? You didn't say so, but I had a feeling that you thought I was crazy when I became engaged to Mae. Maybe I was, but I thought you'd washed out that old rule, single men only. Men wouldn't stay single."

"We washed it out," agreed Craigie. "But we mustn't take risks. If you're worried about Mae, you can't concentrate on this job. We've some more news. Professor Conway was kidnapped this afternoon, and we know where they've taken him. This is a big job, and you're the man for it—I hope."

CHAPTER 3
ORDERS

No one was smiling now.

Ross looked sharply from Craigie to Loftus, and back again. There was no noticeable change in Craigie's manner, or in the big man's, but tension had sprung into the room. Ross didn't try to break it, when he said softly:

"So you let them get him."

"That's right," said Craigie.

"Knowing you might never get him back."

"We'll get him back."

Ross said: "I don't know what's come over you. Conway is the man who matters most. We all know that. You might have been justified in taking risks with some of the other back-room boys, but not with Conway. And you can calmly sit there and tell me you know where he's gone, and my job is to get him back. If they've taken Conway, they'll never let him escape alive."

"Losing confidence?" Loftus asked.

"Just dealing in facts. It was crazy."

Craigie said: "We're at a disadvantage, Peter, because we have to use men who're still human beings first and agents afterwards. These people don't. We don't know yet who they are, but we do know they've been trying to get at the air-defence plans of Great Britain, and we also know that those plans include some nifty new inventions and part of the answer to atomic warfare. They include a serum which proofs the human body against radioactive elements, too. They're vital to our defences. Conway is a five-star genius in this line, but there are other five-star men—three of them working with Conway on this job. His loss would be a nasty blow, but wouldn't be fatal. It would be fatal if he were to pass on anything he knows—and we can't be sure what kind of pressure he'll have to withstand. The wise thing is to assume that he'll talk under pressure. He mustn't talk."

Ross didn't speak. He looked older, and his eyes seemed dark, yet appeared to be burning.

"Understand?" asked Craigie.

"Yes, I get it. You let them take Conway while I was off duty for a breather, and now you want me to get him back—which is a nice way of saying you want me to kill him, because he might talk. A fine job for a so-called Secret Service man—to kill one of our brighter scientists."

"You will probably rescue him alive."

"You know I shan't," said Ross.

"If you or anyone else starts out with the conviction that he's bound to fail, failure's round the corner. We want you keyed up to do the impossible, Peter." Craigie spoke very quietly. "We've known that Miss Harrison wasn't too happy about your disappearances on this imaginary test flying, but we didn't know that she would precipitate a crisis when the job's just getting properly under way."

"You forgot you were dealing with human beings."

"We don't have a chance to forget it," Craigie said. He was quiet and almost casual, showing no sign of strain. "Harry Marshall had the job of watching Conway this afternoon—he's now in the mortuary at Scotland Yard, killed by a car near Hyde Park Corner."

Ross tightened his lips, and there was a long silence.

"We'd had Harry covered, or we shouldn't know where Conway was taken, but the shadow couldn't get early word to us as well as watch Conway all the time," Craigie went on at last. "We received a message a little too late. Now we must get Conway back. Can you give your whole mind to it?"

Ross stood up.

"Does Sybil Marshall know?"

"About Harry?" Loftus broke in. "No. I'm going to see her later."

"I'll go," said Ross. "I know her better." He stood with his back to the fireplace, and helped himself to another whisky and soda. "Listen, the two of you. Mae doesn't think I'm a test pilot, and she's mad because I leave so often at short notice. She's no fool, and when she makes up her mind to do a thing, she usually does it. Well, I'll go and see Sybil and then Mae, and tell Mae I shall be out of the country for a bit. That might keep her from probing too far. Now tell me as much as you can about this place where they've taken Conway, I'll need to spend a lot of time studying that."

"It's a river-side bungalow near Shepperton," Craigie said. "It's in a turning to the left off the main road, about a mile and a half after Sunbury. The signpost is marked River Lane. There's a motor launch tied up at the jetty and two fast cars in the garage. They may try to take Conway off tonight, to get him out of the country."

"Sure he's intended to leave the country?"

"We aren't sure of anything."

Ross laughed; it didn't sound funny.

"You're a pretty good pair! Anyone would think there was all the time in the world. Cancel my trip to Sybil, cancel the second visit to Mae. How do you know Conway hasn't been taken off already?"

"The bungalow's being watched."

"And if they make a move before I get there?"

"We don't intend to let them take Conway out of the country alive," said Craigie. "It's the Devil's own job, but we think you're the most likely man to get him back unhurt."

"Who's on the job at the bungalow?"

"Perry, Williamson, and Brown."

"They'll be under your orders when you arrive," said Loftus. "Want anyone else?"

"How many residents at the bungalow?"

"Two men known, plus Conway, and we haven't had a report that anyone else has arrived. Some might."

"Four of us ought to be enough," said Ross. "Better have a couple of reserves to throw in, in case things get rough. Usual terms?"

"You're on your own, and you can use your own judgement," said Craigie. "Just get Conway back."

"Strike the medal ready for me," said Ross, and laughed again, on the same hard note. "When are you going to tell me everything?"

"We have."

"These people aren't Russians?"

"They're certainly not Russians, and we haven't anything to suggest that they're Reds," said Craigie. "Just someone who has been trying to get at our air-defence plans for some time—and who've killed two of our best men in the process. You know as much as we do, Peter." He stood up. "Good luck."

"I'll need it," Ross said. He looked at the whisky bottle, shook his head, lit a cigarette, and went to the wall, which seemed quite blank. "Do your magic, Gordon."

Craigie stretched out his right hand and pressed a button in the mantelpiece; immediately the door in the wall slid open. Ross put his hand to his forehead in a mock salute, and went out; he didn't look back as the doors closed behind him.

"He'll do it," said Craigie.

"He'll try." Loftus poked his fingers through his hair. "This Mae is quite a little lady."

"He'll put her out of his mind for the next few hours."

"But not indefinitely," Loftus said. "You know it as well as I do. We've been watching him as if he were our own son, and there's serious trouble there. Know the way I think we can keep Ross in the game?"

"What?"

"Bring Mae in with him. She measures up to everything."

"Let's see how it goes tonight," said Craigie.

There was a lull in the traffic in Whitehall when Ross reached it, and London seemed quiet beneath the stars of early May. He could still see the pale shape of the Cenotaph, and the massive squatness of the Ministry buildings. There were few people about, and a string of empty taxis passed him. He walked rapidly towards a side street until he was off the main road and, a few yards along, stopped at a long-nosed Humber Snipe, a gleaming black beauty beneath the light of a street lamp and the yellow glow from the window of a club. A man with a bald head stood with his back to the window.

Ross got into the car and started off, but he did not put on speed until the car was clear of Victoria. Then he tossed his cigarette out of the window and really moved. He passed everything on the road, including three indignant policemen, who undoubtedly tried to take his number, and headed for Putney. He slowed down and watched the headlights of another car behind him, a car which had been keeping pace with him for the past mile. It slackened speed. He grinned into the driving-mirror, and trod on the accelerator again, took a corner sharply, swung into a side road, and then jammed on his brakes. A minute later, the other car flashed past the end of this road. Ross waited for two more minutes, turned the car and went back to the main road, taking another route. He had been going for ten minutes, when he saw the headlights of a car behind him, slowed down, and found that the other car also slowed down.

He didn't like it.

He didn't try to shake the other driver off immediately, except by putting on speed; the Humber had plenty, but the other driver had no difficulty in keeping pace, and lay about a hundred yards behind. Ross swung off the main road into a lane, and waited again, in darkness. He heard the whine as the other car passed. He gave it five minutes this time, then crept out on to the main road. Two or three cars were in sight, but none with the same powerful headlights as the car which had been following him. He travelled at fifty miles an hour and seemed to be crawling, but he wasn't followed.

He let himself think—of Conway.

He knew that Craigie and Loftus, as the leaders of Department Z, had the single duty of counter-espionage in England. He knew them well, had worked with them on and off for years, starting with a job during the war, when he had been parachuted into Occupied France. He knew that the Department was good; that it had worked miracles and achieved the impossible—chiefly because the need for miracles was constantly thrust upon it.

He knew why they gave him top marks.

He was the secretive type; that had started from brooding in early boyhood, and the war had got rid of the brooding without dispensing with the secretiveness. He had always known what he wanted and set out to get it with a single-mindedness of purpose which Craigie and Loftus often found necessary. He usually obtained what he wanted—as, two months ago, he had obtained Mae.

He cut the thought out of his mind.

He thought of Harry Marshall on a cold stone bench, and of Sybil, his wife—then put that out of his mind, also.

Professor Conway was brilliant, too brilliant to lose. Atomic weapons and defence against them were the most vital military factors. Craigie had hellish tasks to execute, which meant that he had to give hellish orders. There was no doubt that the Powers That Be had ordered Conway to be killed rather than taken out of England alive. It was ruthless, as the Department was often ruthless, and it might have to be done.

But not if he could help it.

He thought of Perry, Williamson, and Brown—good men, who would take orders unquestioningly and carry them out no matter what it cost; but when they were standing easy, they would behave like undergraduates on a spree. When it came to the point, he could fool as easily as they could—the difference was that they enjoyed it, he didn't. He knew that none of them was a key agent, and was never likely to be. In a way he envied them; it was easier just to do what you were told. He was putting it too high; in emergency they would show plenty of initiative, but they were useful chiefly because their reflexes worked well and—like Harry—they'd take the last count without complaint.

It was hard to believe that Harry was dead.

And Conway's kidnappers had killed him; that gave a second good reason for wanting to do some damage tonight. He slackened speed and lit a cigarette, then went all out—only to slow down suddenly again. He dropped the cigarette out of the window.

The car was behind him again.

The driver must have missed him, come this far and then waited in a side road until he'd passed.

He was near an A.A. box, stopped and went across to it, opened it with his key and called Craigie's office. He said laconically that he was being followed, and:

"Not by one of us, is it?"

"No," Loftus answered. "Take it easy, Peter."

"Oh, sure," said Ross. "I just wanted to know. Bye." He rang off and sauntered back to the car. The other car was some distance off, parked at the side of the road, with the headlights dipped. Ross started off again, reached a wide curve and, swiftly, swung round in the road, reversed and was off again in the other direction, almost without stopping. The other car was only thirty or forty yards away, and Ross drove at it, his headlights blazing. The car was forced to pull to one side, hit the verge, bumped over it, and then crashed against the hedge; the engine stalled. Ross parked his car and rushed towards the big car, gun in his right hand. He expected shooting, but it didn't come; was the driver stunned? He reached the side of the car, and saw the driver sitting erect—a vague figure in the gloom, but not so vague that he couldn't see that it was a woman.

The window was open.

"Just keep still," Ross said, then stretched out his free hand and opened the door. "Now let me have a look at you."

The woman turned to face him.

"So, as you couldn't get away from me, you'll try to kill me," said Mae.

CHAPTER 4
RIVER-SIDE

"You get the most wonderful ideas," Ross said. He helped her out of the car. There was no other traffic in sight, and he climbed in, backed the car from the hedge, found that there was no serious damage, and pulled up on the verge; no one passing would think they were in trouble. Mae stood and watched him, without speaking. He took the keys of her car, locked the doors, slid the keys into his pocket, and led Mae, hand on her elbow, to his own car.

They got in.

"Darling," said Mae, "I didn't know you were a Sphinx."

"What makes you so interested in the man you're not going to marry?"

"I warned you," said Mae.

"That's right, but you haven't answered me."

"I want to know if she's blonde or brunette."

"Just jealousy," mused Ross, and let in the clutch. "You'll be surprised where it can lead you, precious. How did you manage to find out where I was?"

"I just followed you."

"You didn't. Not in London."

"Oh, that," said Mae. "I followed you one night last week and saw you park the car outside the club, and then saw you go through that little door. So tonight I went straight to the parking-place. I was there when you arrived, and you didn't seem to notice you were being followed until we were out of the traffic. After that, I was lucky."

"How?"

"You could have taken several other roads, but you chose this. So did I."

"Why?"

"Call me psychic," said Mae.

"You ought to be a policewoman," said Ross. "Or else a private detective. You wouldn't need any lessons in following crooks in cars."

"But you're not a crook, are you, darling?"

"Not yet," said Ross. "I'm not even wanted for murder or wife-beating."

He started up the car, turned it and drove slowly along, keeping a look-out for the signpost about which Gordon had told him.

"It's going to be wonderful, when we're married," said Mae.

"You gave me back the ring, remember? I don't have to give you a second chance."

"How gallant, Peter dear."

Ross said quietly: "Mae, listen. I told you I was on hush-hush work, and you ought to have had the common sense to know I wasn't lying about that. We can get through most of the trials of marriage if we've a basis of mutual trust. If we haven't, there's no point in going on with it. I ought to be savagely angry with you, and it wouldn't take much to make me feel that way. I'm on an important job, and I can't risk distractions."

"How high will you fly?" asked Mae sweetly.

"You didn't have to take the flying literally, you just had to realise that I was on secret work, and sit back and wait until it was over."

"I'm not the sit-at-home-and-darn-socks kind, Peter."

"You don't have to darn socks. You could knit."

Mae didn't answer.

Ross said: "I've told you more than I have before, and more than I ought to have. Just at the moment you're in the way. And more—you're a menace. I've one thing to think about, and distractions might make me careless. If I'm careless, I might get hurt."

She drew in her breath.

Ross caught sight of the white signpost, with River Lane painted on it in black. He turned off the main road. A little farther along a car was parked at the side of the road; this was a popular spot for courting couples. The red light of this car was in the shape of a diamond, and Ross knew that its passengers were the 'reserves' for whom he had asked. He saw neither of them.

"Peter, just what are you doing?" Mae asked.

"If I have to tell you in words of three letters, you aren't the girl I thought you were." Ross slowed down. "It's dangerous and it's hush-hush, and this is probably the last time I shall be working on it—and not because of your fervent wish. I'll get the sack." He sounded bitter, and his voice was hard and uncompromising. "It happens to be a job I think is important, and I've a pride in my work. You've done very nicely to-night."

"I'm sorry, Peter." Mae sounded almost humble; that wasn't like her.

"You needn't be sorry. You've opened my eyes to a part of you I didn't know existed, and I don't like it."

The car stopped.

"Peter…"

"I won't be any use to my Chief with a beautiful doll fastened round my neck," Ross said. "He can't take the risk of using a man who'll be followed around by a woman searching for imaginary blondes. But you're not going to spoil tonight's job, precious, it matters. This is where we get out."

"Peter!"

"Come on," he said.

She slid across the front of the seat and got out. Except for the stars and the sidelights of the car behind them, it was dark. He could only just see the pale blur of her face, and the night breeze wafted the perfume she was wearing—subtle, intoxicating—but it didn't affect him. He took her elbow, and they walked along the gravel road towards the other car. Not until they were ten feet away from it did Mae stop.

"Where are we going?"

"My friends are going to look after you," Ross said.

"Friends? A couple of…"

A man climbed out of the other car, another on the far side. Mae stopped. One man showed tall and lean against the sky-line, and there was only one man in Department Z with that lanky figure; his name was Lane. The man struck a match, ostensibly to light a cigarette, actually to show Ross his face.

"Hallo, Peter? Want any help?"

"I don't but my friend does," said Ross. "This is Mae Harrison, and she was stranded along the road—her car broke down. Take her back to Hampton, will you, and put her on the first non-stop train that comes in—for Waterloo. Not a stopping train, she's in a great hurry."

"Delighted," said Wally Lane.

"Then telephone a garage to pick up her car, along the road—a black Lagonda—and drive it to Waterloo. She can pick it up there. Then come back and wait here, please. One of you stay here all the time," said Ross, as an afterthought.

"Right," said the man from the other side of the car, a shorter and stockier man who had not lit a cigarette.

"Mae, this is Wally Lane, an old friend of mine," said Ross. "You'll get along fine, I should think. Make quite sure Mae doesn't miss the train, Wally, won't you?"

"My dear chap! I'll keep closer than a brother."

"Thanks." Ross turned to Mae. "Good night, precious, sleep well."

He swung round.

"Peter!"

He didn't respond to her cry, and went straight to his car. Before he had started the engine, the other car had started up, and the driver began to reverse. Ross wiped the sweat from his forehead, took a flask from the dashboard recess and gave himself a nip of whisky. He didn't relax, felt taut as a tension cable. He'd felt savage and been savage with Mae, and there wasn't any way of being sure that he'd used the right methods. Being soft wouldn't help with Mae, but this might cut her too deep. He'd meant what he said, but knew he would probably regret much of it in the morning.

He had to forget it.

He drove on slowly, and soon reached the river. The road ran alongside it, and the stars reflected from the smooth surface, showing the trees on the far bank more clearly and the bungalows that were dotted along, most of them close to the water. Shepperton itself lay some distance ahead, but the bungalow where Professor Conway was prisoner was somewhere along here. He saw several jetties jutting out into the river, there were lights on at some of the windows, radio music blared from one bungalow, a dizzy South American tune was in sharp contrast to the calmness and quiet loveliness of this night scene. Close at hand, Ross could see the water lapping gently against the bank. A hundred yards away, a car was parked at the back of one of the bungalows—all of which fronted the river. The road was poor, with deep ruts in it, and the car jolted from side to side. He switched off his headlights as he crawled towards the parked car, and a man came from it.

Ross stopped.

"Peter?"

It was Williamson, a man about his own size and figure.

"Hallo, Tim."

"Hallo. No birds flown?"

"No, he's still here. Another Johnny arrived half an hour ago, that makes at least three plus the Professor," said Williamson. "There may be others in there."

"Where's Perry?"

"Squatting in a little launch in the jetty next to the one we're interested in, so that he can hoot like an owl or make a noise like a goldfish if they leave by the front and try to sneak off in their motor launch. What a launch! High-powered beauty, and worth a fortune. A funny thing happened to it."

Ross found himself grinning.

"What?"

"Something to do with the petrol lead," said Williamson apologetically. "Perry fixed it, he's the engineer of the party. He says that if they do start off that way, they won't get more than a couple of miles, and then the engine will go pop-pop-pop-pop, and Bob's your uncle."

"Not bad," murmured Ross. "Where's Brown?"

"Sitting in another car, three gardens removed—just round the corner, we can't see it from here. He has cushions, trust him to get an easy job. The bungalow where they've got Conway is the next but one to this—with the red light in the inside window."

Ross had already seen the window, which was long and narrow; light came through a thin red curtain and spread a pallid glow over a little stretch of the garden. The bungalow was fifty yards from where he had parked, and he couldn't be seen from it.

"Haven't they posted any guards?"

"Nary a sentinel," said Williamson, and stifled a yawn. "They're over-confident, my boy, they don't think anyone knows where they are. That was Perry, he shadowed them. Heard about Harry Marshall?"

The tone of Williamson's voice didn't alter.

"Yes."

"What's the drill?" asked Williamson.

"We want Conway alive, and Gordon thinks they'll kill him rather than let him go. The one certain thing is they mustn't get him away alive."

"Not much fear of that," said Williamson. "I don't quite catch on, Peter. They've tucked up for the night, as far as I can see, don't seem to have any idea of leaving suddenly— garage locked, cars inside, it's true they could use the launch, but Perry says there isn't enough petrol in the tank for thirty miles, so they haven't fuelled for a long journey. Some kind of hoax, I wonder?"

"Not over-confidence?"

"Could be. But they're good—very good. This doesn't seem to measure up to their usual standard."

"No," agreed Ross thoughtfully. "It doesn't measure up, but there's no reason to think they're slipping. What fast one could they pull?"

"Helicopter?" asked Williamson, and gave an inane little laugh.

"I suppose it's possible, but I shouldn't think it's likely."

Ross took the suggestion seriously, was prepared to accept any possibility. The most likely thing was that the kidnappers thought they were safe, that no one dreamt they were here, and that their only concern was keeping Conway quiet. They'd want Conway alive, so he was in no immediate danger, but if they were attacked what would happen? Conway would be shot—they wouldn't allow him to be recaptured. Without knowing it, Conway was going to be shot from both sides.

"Dark thoughts?" Williamson asked.

"Gloomy," agreed Ross. "The problem's simple—to get him without being hurt, but although they may think they're safe, they won't take any chances inside."

"Meaning, they'll kill him rather than…"

"That's it."

Williamson said: "Couldn't we stage an accident just outside, and go there to beg for help? If they're sure they're not suspected, they'd probably fall for it. The simple things often come off."

"I don't like it," Ross said. "The whole set-up seems phoney."

Williamson shrugged.

Ross opened the door of the car and got out, glancing up and down. The radio music was muffled by the distance, but he could still hear it. With the engine switched off, he could hear the lapping of the waves against the river-bank. Everything seemed simple and straightforward, he might be imagining uncertainty and menace. Nine times out of ten, a raid came off without any trouble, but the gravest risk was that Conway would be killed.

Ross knew that he was in a bad mood. He didn't consciously dwell on that last meeting with Mae, but it bit deeply into his subconscious, and he wasn't easy about it.

"Don't leave it too late," Williamson said. "We mustn't disturb the Professor's beauty sleep."

"Listen," said Ross. "They catch one of the biggest plums they're after, they bring him to a sleepy little bungalow in a lonely little spot, and do precisely nothing—no guard in the grounds, no one at the windows, no interest taken in what goes on. I tell you it doesn't add up. We've missed some of the numbers. What would you do, if you'd kidnapped Conway and brought him here?"

"Bristle with guards," said Williamson promptly.

"Where would you put them?"

Williamson put his head on one side.

"Hang it, old chap."

He sounded forlorn.

"You might put them in the obvious place, in the garden or at the windows, or you might say that would be too obvious. But you'd have them about, and make quite sure you knew if there was any raid in the offing." He looked at the bungalow next to that with the red curtain. "In there, for instance. The other one could be a decoy hide-out."

"Hum," said Williamson, and sounded impressed.

The other bungalow was in darkness.

"Seen anyone there?"

"No. There hasn't been a light on, I took it for granted that the place was empty. A lot of these places are used for week-ends and holidays, you know, not by permanent residents."

"Supposing we find out," said Ross.

CHAPTER 5
FORCED ENTRY

"What's the size of it?" Williamson asked, as they stood looking at the darkened bungalow. "Walk straight up and knock at the door?"

"If there's anyone inside, they'll know we're here, and they'll probably guess why," said Ross. "We're out of sight of the main bungalow, but not this one."

"My fool fault."

"No one's fault yet, I may be dreaming," said Ross. "I think we'll both drive off. If they're in this place they're not likely to be near the one where Brown's parked, and shouldn't know anything about him or Perry."

"We took all precautions," Williamson said, with a faint note of laughter. "We shove off, and they think we've given up or gone for help, is that it?"

"You're catching on," said Ross, amiably.

"Going to tell the others?"

"Not yet."

Ross went back to his car, reversed in the narrow road, and swung away, towards the main road and the spot where he had sent Mae off. Williamson followed shortly afterwards, and they drove at speed for several minutes before

Ross slowed down. Williamson reversed, and Ross joined him in his car, a Lagonda.

"We'll drive back without lights, stop fifty yards away, and walk the rest," said Ross.

The bungalow was still in darkness when they got out of the car. By standing on one side of the road, they could see the red glow from the window of the other. There was grass at the side of the road, and they walked quickly, without making any noise. Perry and Brown would realise that they were manoeuvring, would stay under cover until there was obvious need for them.

Everything was quiet.

They reached the side of the dark bungalow, and Ross climbed over the low wooden fence which surrounded the garden. Williamson, nearly as tall as the man who was escorting Mae, made easy work of it. The walls were pale-coloured, and showed up in the starlight; there was a dark patch, of a doorway, almost opposite them. They reached it, then saw a flash of light through a small window.

Ross held Williamson's arm tightly.

Neither man spoke.

They reached the window, and stood to one side, peering in. A door was open slightly, and the light came from a passage or a room beyond. A man passed. There was a sharp ringing sound, as of a telephone bell.

"Could be sweet innocents having an early night and disturbed by the telephone," Williamson whispered.

"Could be."

Ross stepped to the door—the tradesman's door. There were two cement steps leading up to it, but there was no porch, and the door was of solid wood. He shone a pencil torch on the keyhole, and examined it closely, then took out a knife and picked a blade open; it was a skeleton key.

Williamson stood some way off, watching the front door—the one facing the river.

From his position Ross could see no light inside, and after the first sharp ring there had been no sound. Metal scraped softly on metal, yet seemed loud in the quiet. Ross felt the key grip, and turned gently; if it slipped and clicked loudly, it might be heard inside. He was on edge, and he shouldn't be; normally, he took a thing like this in his stride.

The lock clicked back, not loudly.

He waited; nothing stirred in the bungalow.

Williamson came back.

"Nothing doing out there."

"We'll go in."

Ross pushed the door gently, afraid that it would squeak; the only sound was from the bottom of the door, where it caught against a rug or a carpet. He opened it wide enough to step through. The faint light showed the tiles and the chromium plating of a modern kitchen; three gleaming taps were above the sink by the window. They stepped towards another door, in a corner; it was unlocked.

From the other side, a man said, "Sure, that's okay."

Were there two people in the bungalow?

They waited, hoping to hear an answer, but there was none. Ross opened the second door, and a faint light shone through. He stepped into a narrow passage. Two doors led off this, and one was open; the light came from there.

A man laughed, on a low note.

"Don't you worry."

There was no response.

Ross slid his right hand into his pocket and crept towards the open door. There was a carpet, muffling the sound of his movements. Williamson was like a shadow, just behind him.

There was a ting! as of a telephone receiver being replaced. The man laughed again.

"They take some convincing."

"Well, we saw the beggars go, and haven't seen them come back."

"We saw them all right," said the first man, "and we'll hear if they drive back. How's the little lady?"

"Don't worry about her."

"Sure I'm going to worry about her," the first man said. His English was good, he was undoubtedly a native. "She's worth worrying about." A shadow appeared in the hall, and then a man with his hand on the side of the door. "I'm just going to kiss her good night."

Ross had backed away, and stood, still as death, in a doorway. Williamson had backed into the kitchen. More light showed a burly man in his shirt-sleeves, who crossed the passage without looking right or left and stood by another door, with a key in his hand. Ross heard the key turn, and the man laugh again as he stepped into the room beyond. He switched on another light, and said:

"Hallo, duckie, glad to see me?"

There was no answer.

He stepped inside, and pushed the door to, without quite closing it. Ross motioned to Williamson, who could now see him in the better light. Ross pointed towards the room from which the man had come, and Williamson went towards it softly, while Ross went to that where the burly man had gone. They made no sound, were at their respective doors without being seen.

They kicked each door wider open, as if worked by a time switch; and there were guns in their hands.

A small, tough-looking man, with a wriggly nose and eyebrows which jutted out like a young forest, was standing by a table in the room where Williamson went. He swung round as the door opened, gaping, round-eyed. He made a gurgling noise in his throat—and then leapt towards the telephone. Williamson reached him in two strides, and struck him savagely on the side of the head. The man's right hand clawed the telephone, but didn't take off the receiver. Williamson hit him again, and he slumped to the floor.

"Sorry," said Williamson mildly. "Just pipe down, little man."

Ross stepped into the other room, a bedroom, as the burly man heard the kick and turned swiftly. The man's right hand went to his pocket in a flash, but he wasn't as quick as Ross, who reached and struck him with the butt of the gun. He caught the man on the temple, dodged a whirling blow from the other's left fist, and hit him again, where it hurt. The attack was as swift and sudden as Williamson's; and more thorough, for the burly man groaned as he hit the floor, and lost consciousness. His feet twisted for a moment, and the fingers of his right hand scrabbled on the floor, then became still.

There was a girl on the bed.

She was bound hand and foot, and her feet were also tied to a post of the single bedstead. A scarf was tied round her mouth, gagging her, and her blue eyes were wide open and staring at Ross, as if in terror. The light shone straight into them, and they had a bewildering blueness; her dark hair was almost black.

She lay there, rigid.

The man on the floor didn't stir.

"All right?" called Williamson.

"Fine."

"I'm just going to have a little chat," the other Department Z agent said.

"Do that." Ross smiled at the girl, suddenly; he relaxed for the first time for what seemed hours. "All over, you needn't worry," he said.

He took out his knife again, and cut the cords at her wrists, then gently through the white scarf at her lips. When it fell away, she lay quite still; there were deep ridges on either side of her mouth, which stayed open, it was so stiff. That meant she had been there for some time. Ross cut the cords at her ankles, slid an arm beneath her shoulders, eased her up to a sitting position, and put pillows behind her. He kept smiling, and it wasn't the hard, brittle smile which others knew. There was a softness in it, gentleness which Mae would have found unusual, because he was generally intent with her; or flippant.

"No need to worry at all, or to talk until you're easier," he said. There was a full carafe and a glass at the side of the bed, and he poured out a little water and put the glass to her lips. These moved for the first time, but most of the water dribbled down her chin and on to her white blouse.

She wore just a blouse and a light-grey skirt—her shoes were at the side of the bed, one upright, one on its side. A pearly brooch was pinned to the top of the white blouse—small and round. Her dark hair was a tumbled mass of unruly waves. She was very pale, and perhaps that heightened the blueness of her eyes; he had never seen such eyes.

"Just take it easy," he said.

He glanced at the burly man, who hadn't stirred.

"I'll take him away—be back in a jiffy."

Even his voice was more gentle.

The burly man didn't open his eyes when Ross took his legs and dragged him out of the room. Williamson was talking to the man in the other room, and as Ross backed into it, he heard the agent say:

"So that's the lot—three men and the Professor, next door."

"Yes!"

The man with the wriggly nose was sitting on the edge of a chair, his lips parted, his eyes shadowed with terror. Williamson held his right wrist, but did not appear to be exerting any pressure. He glanced at the other prisoner, and gulped.

"Doing all right?" Ross asked.

"Not so badly, Peter. Our kind friend says that he and his buddy were watching to see if there was any trouble for the household next door. Conway's there, with three boy friends. And the buddy has just telephoned to report that we've gone away, and that there's no immediate danger. They plan to move out at midnight, we've plenty of time."

"Not bad," murmured Ross. "Hold his arm still."

He took a small narrow box from his breast pocket, took off the lid—and a hypodermic syringe gleamed in the light of the small sitting-room. The man in the chair began to shout, and Williamson spread one large hand over his face, stifling the cry, and still held his wrist. Ross jabbed the needle in, then turned to the man on the floor. He turned up the shirt-sleeve of the right arm, and the needle went in again—he used half of the shot in each.

"How long will it take to slug them?" asked Williamson.

"Five minutes. Will you stay?"

Ross went out, and waved to the girl on the bed, then went through the other rooms; there were six in all, and no one else was in the bungalow. It was cheaply furnished, as a week-end chalet might be, with hair carpet on the floor.

When he finished, the man in the chair was leaning back with his eyes closed.

"Nearly bye-byes," said Williamson. "And the boys next door think they're sitting pretty for the moment. Shall I tell Brown and Perry?"

"Will you? We'll close in at"—Ross glanced at his wristwatch—"eleven o'clock. Mine says twenty minutes to, check yours and the others, will you?"

"Right, sir!"

Williamson patted the head of the man with the wriggly nose, who took no notice of it and was more relaxed than when Ross had returned. Ross lifted his right eyelid; there was no doubt that the injection had taken effect.

They would be unconscious for at least two hours.

Ross brushed his hair back, smoothing it from his forehead, and turned round. The two doors were open, but the girl couldn't see into this room because the head of the bed was in the wrong position. Ross could see her legs—slim and shapely; she wore silk stockings, not nylon. He caught himself out smiling as he went across and stood in the doorway. He raised his hand.

"Feeling better?"

"Yes—thank you."

Speaking was obviously painful, but the terror had faded from her eyes.

"Fine! We'll soon have you out of here."

He went towards her, smiling, asking himself who she was and what had brought her into this. She looked—good. There was some colour in her cheeks now, and he had been wrong; pink cheeks made the blue in her eyes much brighter and clearer; he reminded himself that he had never seen such eyes. She was slim, too, with a lovely figure.

"Who are you?" she asked hoarsely.

"Police. Who're you?"

"I'm Alice Conway. I think they've kidnapped my father." She spoke jerkily, and fear flared in her eyes. "Is he—*is he here?*"

Chapter 6
The Professor

"No," said Ross, promptly and gently, "but he's not far away, we'll soon get him back. I've some colleagues, they'll be here in ten minutes. Just take it easy, and don't worry about him."

He found it hard to add that rider, because there was plenty of need to worry, and he didn't want to lie to the girl. It was because of her eyes, their colour and the brightness of their intense and anxious gaze.

"Are you—sure?"

Ross smiled. "We dealt with two of them, and the others don't know we're here, it will be easy. When did you get here?"

"This afternoon."

"How come?"

Ross poured out more water and handed it to her.

"I had a message to meet Father at Green Street, Chelsea, that's on the Embankment, near his office. I often meet him there in the car, and we go for a drive. A man came up, and—he had a gun. I had to drive where he told me." She seemed astonished at the ease with which it had been done. We came here, and—I've been on this bed ever since."

She moved her legs slowly towards the side of the bed.

"There's no hurry," said Ross.

"I want to see if I can walk."

He took her arm, and she put her feet on the floor, wincing; he could imagine the pain in them as the blood began to circulate. She leaned against him heavily, and couldn't help herself. He put his right arm round her shoulders; she was warm, soft. Her hair brushed against his face, and he moved his head back.

"Leave this until later," he advised.

She took two faltering steps and stopped; she would have fallen but for his help.

"Are you sure you'll get my father?"

"That's my job."

"But…"

"We found you, didn't we?" asked Ross. He still didn't like lying to her, and couldn't imagine why, if ever there were a white lie, this was it. Then he realised it was because he would hate the task of telling her, if they should fail to get Conway alive.

She didn't look at him, was concentrating on her feet.

"If you must try to walk, look at the wall," said Ross. "Haven't you ever ridden a bicycle? If you stare at the front wheel, you wobble."

She made a funny little sound, which might have been a laugh, then took several steps fairly steadily. After two or three minutes she was able to walk without his assistance. He stood watching her; she was good to look at. She brushed her hair back from her forehead. She had more colour, and the ridges at her mouth had largely gone, leaving two angry red patches. She wasn't beautiful in the sense that Mae was beautiful, but striking; if striking was the word. She had a heart-shaped face and a rather large mouth; too large. Her nose was small and her upper lip very short, and her eyes—he hadn't realised before how large they were, and how the dark lashes curled, the lower ones sweeping her cheek.

There was something the matter with him, he ought to be thinking of her father.

"That's more like it," he said.

"I want to help."

"Eh?"

"I want to help you to get Father."

"Sorry," said Ross. "It's our job. I want you to stay here, in this room, and do——" He broke off. "Wrong! I want you to leave the place and walk towards the main road—just walk, until you come to a car about half a mile along. It should be back by now. There'll be two men in it. Tell them that P.R. would like to see them here as soon as possible, but they are to see you to a place of safety first."

"That'll take ages!"

"They're just reserves," said Ross. "Here's the first eleven."

Williamson came in, smoking a cigarette. He waved his right hand negligently, and although he didn't stare at the girl, Ross knew that he was startled by her looks; or her eyes.

"All set," he said. "Five minutes to go."

"Right." Ross put a hand on the girl's shoulder. "Do exactly what I ask, it's important. It could make a big difference."

She nodded; obviously she didn't want to go, but he thought she would obey the instructions to the letter. He kept a hand on her arm as he went along to the back door, which Williamson had left wide open. Then he watched her walk up the path and turn towards the main road. She was soon hidden from sight, even the pale mark of her white blouse was gone.

"Ready?" asked Williamson.

"Yes. Guess who that is."

"All I know is that you'd normally give her a shot of sleeping-mixture, and make sure she wasn't fooling you," Williamson said. "Who is she?"

Ross felt annoyed, but didn't show it; Williamson was right.

"Conway's daughter."

"Well, well!" breathed Williamson. "I take it all back. Nice little filly, too."

Ross felt more annoyed; and hid it. He was letting his emotions run away with him, wallowing in sickly sentiment, and that wasn't any use for a Department Z man. He had started off on the wrong foot all the evening. Craigie had made a mistake in sending him, someone else ought to have been in charge to-night, he was...

"Now fix Conway as neatly as you did this, and everything will be hunky-dory."

Ross chuckled, and his annoyance faded.

"Thanks, pal," he said lightly. "Now, where are the others?"

They were moving across to the garden of the second bungalow.

"Brown on the far side, opposite this, Perry with the river at his back. I thought I'd take the wall facing the road and you'd take the side entrance, you seem good at picking locks. The rest of us will select a window in advance, and if there's any need, we can smash the window and be with you in a brace of shakes. All this," added Williamson, "because we know you'll want to go in alone. You've three volunteers if you want company."

"I think it's a solo job for a start," said Ross. "Keep your eye on the road, I told the girl to send Wally and Lee along, with luck they'll be here in half an hour. If there's any real trouble, I'll yell—or make sure you know about it somehow."

"We'll be all ears."

Ross nodded, and went towards the side door. This one had a porch, the bungalow was larger and looked more pretentious. He knew that he could be sure that the others would be at their posts and keyed up for any call; they were highly trained, and they would have but one objective: getting Conway alive. He couldn't plan in greater detail; he didn't like a detailed plan, if it went wrong in one respect, it could upset the whole manœuvre.

He started work on the lock of the door. It was a better lock and would take longer to open; it might not be possible to open it. The place next door had been used in the emergency, this was the real prison-house, and there would be more precautions here against burglary. But the people inside were reassured, and felt sure they'd get warning of possible danger.

Metal scraped on metal; it seemed to make more noise than when he'd forced the other lock.

He was touched by a faint red glow from the window, and that was sufficient, he didn't need his torch. He felt perspiration gathering on his forehead, although it wasn't hot; cold sweat was a bad sign. Conway was in here, and Conway mattered. It wasn't only because he was a big man behind the air-defence of the country; it was partly because he was a man whom the Department wanted to get back safely. This was a job which had to be done, and like all Department jobs, it was vitally important while it lasted.

Would Conway be in a room, alone?

Or would one of the men be with him?

He kept twisting and turning the pick-lock, and thought that he would have to try the window. Then the key caught and he twisted quickly; the lock went back, and he pushed the door open an inch. He heard nothing. He waited for half a minute before pushing the door wide open and stepping into the passage. It was easy; as easy as it had been next door, and in its way, too smooth. The moment of greatest danger was when all was going well.

He closed the door softly behind him.

The light was on in the wide hall, and two passages and several doors led off this; it was twice as large as the place next door. The doors were painted white; there were good water-colours on the wall; the floorboards were narrow oak strips, polished and strewn with skin rugs—a snare for the unwary step. Everything here had a touch of quality. He reached the centre of the hall. Lights showed under only two doors—the door of the room with the red curtains and the one to the right of it. He passed this and turned into a passage; there were two more doors here, and each was unlocked; they were empty bedrooms.

He walked back cautiously, making no sound, and tried the other passage, where a bathroom, kitchen, and W.C. were close together. He was now left with the two front rooms. There were no stairs; they would hardly put Conway in the loft.

The loft hatch was in one of the passages.

He went back and studied it; there was no sign that it had recently been opened. Tiny cobwebs hung across, proof that it hadn't been opened that day.

There was only silence and the hall light.

He reached the hall again, and went to the door of the room where there was no light; there had been none at the window, and none showed beneath the door. He tried the handle, but the door was locked. The key wasn't here.

Conway might be inside.

Above everything else, he wanted Conway to be there.

He took out his pick-lock, hesitated, then went towards a mirror which hung fairly high. He put a chair in position, stepped up and lifted the mirror from its hooks and, with great care, stepped down again. His shoe squeaked on the boards, and with the mirror still in his arms, he stood rigid as he stared towards the door.

It didn't open.

He carried the mirror to the corner by the front door, then went to the door he wanted to open. He could see only part of the one behind him, so he altered the position of the mirror; then he could see all of the door. If it began to open, he would have plenty of warning.

He started work with the pick-lock.

Why should they lock the door if the room was empty?

If Conway was in here he would surely be alone, for a guard would want some light.

The noise of metal on metal, already familiar, seemed to grate; how could anyone nearby fail to hear it? He kept glancing at the mirror, but the door remained closed.

The lock clicked; it was the third time he'd heard that sound tonight, and this seemed sharp and loud—the men couldn't fail to hear it. He thrust the door open, met darkness, and stepped swiftly inside. He turned, and kept the door ajar, watching the one opposite; sure that it would open. But it didn't.

If Conway was in this room, then all four men were across the hall.

He felt sick with anxiety.

He stood in the near darkness, hearing the sound of his own breathing, trying to detect that of someone else in the room. He couldn't. He saw the vague shape of the light switch, and pressed it down sharply. Light flooded the room—the empty room. It was a small dining-room, with a long table, six chairs, and a sideboard, with only just space to walk round.

CHAPTER 7
THE BIG ROOM

R oss switched off the light, waited until he was used to the gloom, and stepped towards the window. He had to shift two chairs out of his path, and kicked against a pouf which he hadn't noticed. It made little noise. He reached the window and hesitated, then saw a dark figure loom up outside. He opened the window, which was of the casement type, and Brown, a broad-shouldered barrel of a man, looked at him, his eyes glinting in the starlight.

"Still alive?"

"Just. Tell the others to wait near the red-curtain window, and then come in here and join me, will you?"

"Right!"

There was a note of satisfaction in Brown's hushed whisper.

"Be careful when you walk across the room," Ross said.

He went back, reaching the door and opening it so that he could see into the hall. The other door remained closed, and another thing puzzled him: the silence. It was hard to believe that anyone was here. Would three men sit in absolute silence for so long? There was no apparent reason why they should mute their voices, they could be expected to talk normally. Even if Conway were gagged, the others would talk.

Had he been fooled? Was the light shining in an empty room?

He heard no movement until there was a whisper in his ear.

"All ready," said Brown, who had the uncanny gift of being able to move without a sound.

The silence began to get on Ross's nerves; there was nothing natural about it, he began to feel sure that he would find the room empty. He went through the other rooms in his mind, to make sure that he hadn't left a corner without searching it, and knew that he hadn't. There could be no one else in this bungalow.

The four men *must* be here.

He reached the far door.

"Now?" asked Brown softly.

Ross examined the door, and recalled what he knew of the others in the bungalow. It was solid, and would take a lot of breaking down; but if he tried to pick the lock, men inside would be sure to hear—if any were inside.

The doubt screamed at him, but his hands were steady.

Two shots at the lock would be sufficient to enable one of them to break the door down easily; the other could rush in, gun in hand—it would take only a matter of seconds.

He said: "You fire at the lock, I'll go in."

"Right. Ready?"

"Yes."

Ross drew back.

Brown, standing on one side, levelled his gun at the lock; it was a revolver, not a light automatic, Brown liked weight in his weapons. There was only a fraction of a second's pause before the roar and the flash—and another roar and flash. Brown put his whole weight against the door and thrust, it burst open. Ross went in, crouching low, gun at his waist—and there wasn't a sound or movement from inside the room.

He pulled up.

Four men were here, and he had found Conway. The Professor was sitting back in an arm-chair; he was tied to the arms, by the wrists.

The other three were sitting down, two in chairs, one on a couch. Each appeared to be fast asleep, each was lying back, relaxed and comfortable.

There wasn't a sound.

"What's this?" asked Brown. "Waxworks?"

He had a florid face, a scar over his right eye, short brown hair which stuck up at the back, like a schoolboy's. He was fairly short, but massive and broad across the shoulders. His brown eyes were steady as he surveyed the room, and there was a slight curve of a smile at his lips.

Ross didn't speak.

"Madame Tussaud couldn't do any better," Brown said.

Ross moved across to Conway, his teeth clenched. He did not think there was any doubt about the explanation; these men were dead, all four of them. The mystery of it didn't occur to him, only the shock of the discovery. He reached Conway and stared into the pale, gentle face. Conway didn't seem to be breathing. Ross took his left wrist and felt for the pulse, stood like that while Brown did the same with one of the others—a good-looking man with jet-black hair and eyebrows. Brown dropped his man's arms first.

"Corpus," he announced.

Ross stood rigid, and with the shock receding, hope replacing it; he thought he detected a slight movement. He took his hand away and held his watch close to Conway's mouth; the lips were parted, he could just see part of the big, rather yellow teeth. Brown came across to him.

"Hope?"

Conway didn't stir, but when Ross glanced at the glass of the watch it was smeared faintly.

"Ring the office for a doctor and an ambulance," he said.

There was no sign of life in any of the other men.

This was a large room, delightfully furnished in the modern fashion, with deep arm-chairs, pastel shades of green and yellow, a fitted carpet with many colours in the small pattern. There was a grand piano in a sycamore case, and ornaments which fitted in with the general scheme. The only thing wrong was the curtain at one small window; it was red, looked as if it had been put up in a hurry. It was just a piece of linen. The lighting was mostly concealed, but there were lights over each of six oil-paintings—all of them good.

The handsome man whom Brown had tested first was the youngest; the other two were somewhere in the middle forties. They might have been seen in any London club or any London pub. They were well dressed and looked healthy, it was hard to believe that they were not sleeping; yet there was not the slightest indication of life.

"Let the others in, will you?" asked Ross. He lit a cigarette as he went back to Conway, tried the trick with the watch again, and got the same result; Conway wasn't dead. He looked restful as he lay back there, it was easy to imagine that he had just sat down and fallen asleep. The cords at his wrists weren't tightly tied, and Ross cut them and folded the Professor's arms. Not until the Professor was on a couch, covered with blankets, collar and shoes off, did Ross relax. He was soon trying to get whisky between the set lips, but failed.

Williamson and Perry came in, quickly and quietly.

"All alive-o, then!" Williamson's careful pretence at indifference proved his excitement. "Not bad."

"One alive-o," said Ross. "I don't know what's happened to the others, unless the Professor cast a spell."

"He isn't that kind of Professor, is he?" asked Perry.

He was the smallest man in the room, five-feet-five in height, with a little lithe figure and a keen, thin face and eager grey eyes. He had curly hair which looked rather like a wig, there was so much of it and the waves were so perfect. He was dressed in a faultlessly cut suit of dark brown, and looked almost a dwarf beside Williamson.

"He's not supposed to be that kind of a Professor," Ross said. "This doesn't make…"

"Don't say it." Williamson closed one eye, slowly. "I'll say it for you, it's more my line of kindergarten. Sense. None of it makes sense, but results count, and you've won our prize Professor, he's ready for the bosom of his family again."

"If he lives."

"I wonder if the whisky's poisoned here," said Williamson. "You need a drink."

Ross laughed.

"We won't take any chances with the poison, but we'll use their glasses."

He took out his flask.

As they were drinking, a car pulled up, and the two men who had been on the road came in. The gangling form of Wally, who looked spruce and eager in the bright light of the room, reminded Ross of Mae. He frowned.

"Nice welcome," said Wally. "What have I done to annoy the great one?"

"Idiot. Where's the girl I sent along?"

"I delivered her safe and sound to a policeman who wanted to know what I was doing, parking out there. He was going to take her to his cottage, said his wife would look after her. All right, I hope?"

"Fine. Thanks."

"As for Madame Mae," said Wally with a grin, "she was dulcet sweet all the way. She didn't argue with me once, but left a message—would I tell my friend how sorry she was that she'd interfered."

Ross was eager: "Did she say that?"

"Cross my heart!"

"She's up to something," Ross said, but he laughed. He had been half-afraid that Mae would try to break away from her escort. "I wonder how long that doctor will be."

"A doctor isn't much use with these."

Wally didn't ask questions, didn't even look surprised.

The three men who showed no sign of life were in exactly the same position, half an hour later, when Loftus and a doctor arrived—the doctor a youthful man who did most of the Department's work and was also a police-surgeon attached to Scotland Yard. He was brisk and seemed competent, but he gave no opinion about Conway, except to say that he was alive; the others weren't. Loftus had little to say, and, with Ross, watched the Professor being carried into an ambulance. They stood on the porch as the car was driven off.

Loftus said: "So you managed it."

"It was done for me. Any idea how they were killed?"

"It looks as if they ate or drank something that Conway didn't—or else that didn't affect Conway as much as it did them," said Loftus. "A.B.C. What have you done here?"

"We've looked round." Ross led the way in. "All the papers we've found are on the dining-room table, but we haven't made a full job of it. You're the expert on that. At least we've a couple of live prisoners for you, but they won't come round for a bit."

"They can wait, anyhow," said Loftus. "Going to see Mae?"

Ross laughed, told him what had happened, and also told him about Alice Conway. Loftus made little comment; it was obvious that the girl had been kidnapped so as to exert pressure on her father. The thoroughness of the kidnappings commanded respect; the deaths were simply mysterious.

"Case of the Three Dead Men," Loftus mused. "We'll have the medical report by the time we get back to town. We've plenty of men to handle the job here, Peter—care to take a spell?"

"I think I will," said Ross.

He drove off with Wally Lane, knowing that in the morning he would go over everything that was discovered at the bungalow, and would be brought fully up to date. He drove at a good speed along the by-road, came to the main road a little after midnight, and inquired of a cyclist for the policeman's cottage; it was nearby. There were lights at both the downstairs windows as he drew up, and a policeman's bicycle was leaning against the wall. The front door was open. Wally rang the bell, and a woman bustled out of a room on the right of the passage, small, wiry, curious.

"Good evening, sir, do you want to see the constable? That's my husband, he won't be a minute, he's on the telephone."

"Thanks. Is the young lady still here?"

"Young *lady?*"

Ross felt as if she'd slapped him across the face.

"Yes. The young lady he brought home from the car."

"*My* husband hasn't brought any young lady home, sir."

She was emphatic.

There was a ting, as of the receiver being replaced, and a big man in uniform, without his helmet, loomed large in a doorway.

"Tom, there's a gentleman inquiring about a young lady."

"What young lady?" asked the constable.

Ross said: "You spoke to two men who were in a parked car at the next by-road, and told them you'd look after the young lady who was with them."

"Not me, sir," said the constable. "There's some mistake, *I* haven't spoken to anyone in a car tonight, and I certainly haven't seen any young lady."

CHAPTER 8
LOST ALICE

Wally Lane looked at the constable, and shook his head slowly.

"Not my man, Peter. My chap was taller and not so—er—plump."

"What other policemen live near here?"

Ross's voice was sharp, his eyes glinted.

"None," said the constable firmly. "The next nearest is in Shepperton and after that in Chertsey. There certainly wouldn't be another policeman on duty in this part of the world tonight, not that I know of. Unless it was a patrol car?"

He looked hopefully at Wally.

"No. Cyclist."

"I just can't understand it, sir," said the constable. "It must have been someone *pur*porting to be a police-officer. That's a very serious offence, and I must report it at once. I suppose you're sure?"

He looked almost suspiciously at Wally.

Wally grinned.

"Hardly a sip of alcohol to-night, officer! I can walk the plank, say ipecacuanha wine and indivisible dirigible and pontifical pomposity like one o'clock. Stone cold sober. Peter, I don't like it."

"Excuse me, gentlemen," said the constable, "but I must please ask you to explain what this is all about. Who *are* you?"

Ross didn't answer. He seemed to be looking at a pair of astonishingly bright blue eyes.

Wally showed his Special Branch card, carried by all agents when on normal business, which gave him Scotland Yard authority. The local P.C. passed through the emotions of surprise, consternation, eagerness to impress and to help, and poured out a torrent of not very useful information. At Ross's dictation, he asked his Superintendent to put out a general police call for Alice Conway. Ten minutes later, Ross took the wheel of his car, and Wally sat by him, offering cigarettes.

"Do you get it?" he asked.

"It's coming," said Ross. "A third group."

"We don't even know who the first people are yet."

'That's right,' said Ross, and gave a short laugh. "I think I'd better go back and see Loftus."

A lock of dark hair hung over Loftus's dark eye, the rest of his hair was untidy, ash powdered his coat, and his suit was almost shapeless. When Ross arrived he was standing by a small table in one of the bedrooms, looking through some papers which had been found there. He turned when he heard Ross, walked slowly to the bed, and sat down heavily. He stretched his right leg straight out in front of him; it was artificial, and served to make him ungainly in movement.

"Now what, Peter?"

"Found anything?"

"Not a sausage. We know the owner of the bungalows now, and that they were let furnished, two months ago, to a Mr. Ronald Smith. Mr. Smith is dead—he was the man who took Conway from St. James's Park this afternoon. He's been in and out of this place for some time, but seldom stayed more than two or three days at a stretch. He had a bank account at Staines and another in London, and seemed to be worth a few thousand—beyond that, nothing. You?"

Ross didn't answer, and Loftus frowned.

"Not Mae again?"

Ross grinned crookedly.

"I'm ringing the changes. Alice Conway has been kidnapped."

Loftus whistled softly.

Ross said: "Wally Lane handed her over to a man who looked like a policeman but wasn't. I've had a general call put out for her, and had a word with the Yard myself, from the local copper's house. It looks as if the phoney policeman was keeping a look-out, knew we were going to raid the bungalow, and…"

He broke off.

"Take it steadier," suggested Loftus mildly.

"All right," said Ross, and sat on a chair, its back in front of him, and leaned forward, cigarette jutting from his lips. "We'll make it simple. A group of men known as Y kidnapped Conway and his daughter, because they can learn a lot about our air-defences from Conway. Right?"

"Right."

"Law and order, in the form of Department Z, knew a little about this group. Too little."

Loftus nodded, owlishly.

"There was a third party, whom we'll call X. X was watching the first group, saw that the second group was going to attack, and acted on his own. He needed an excuse for being in the district, and he needed some authority, so he dressed himself up as a policeman."

Again Loftus nodded.

"He had no love for Group Y, had access to their head-quarters, at this bungalow, and poisoned them. As he's snatched Alice Conway, he presumably wants to high-pressure her father, so he wouldn't want her father dead. That's why Conway is alive and the others aren't. Right?"

"Not a foot wrong," said Loftus. "We'll tackle the prisoners on it."

Ross grinned.

"Thank you, sir! It is possible that Group Y and Mr. X were at one time working together, and that X thought it would pay him to work on his own—in other words, that he ratted on Group Y. Someone they knew would find it easier to poison Group Y than someone they didn't know. Whether that's true or not, X is still out to bring pressure on Conway. He hadn't a chance to get him away, as we were around, but he had luck with the girl, and will now try to exert pressure through Conway's daughter. He must have been pretty smart, to have snatched Alice Conway as he did."

"Brilliant," agreed Loftus.

"Until tonight, we knew a little about Group Y, but nothing at all about Mr. X—all we know about Mr. X is that he's clever and quick and that he was expecting us here tonight."

"We have to find out plenty more about him," said Loftus. "You've finished this job, how about having a shot at Mr. X? He'll almost certainly have a stab of some kind at Conway soon, we should get something on him. You cut out everything else, and just think of Mr. X."

"Suits me," said Ross.

"The air-defences are still under fire, and we still don't know who's behind it," Loftus added.

Ross leaned forward and stubbed out his cigarette on a nearby ash-tray.

"Bill, why not admit the obvious—that it's Russia?"

"Because we don't know that's true, and we can't afford to trust the obvious," said Loftus. "You know as well as I do that this might be a private group of spies. Supposing they beat us and discovered everything Conway knows, got possession of the vital air-defence plans? They'd be able to sell to the highest bidder. Our Government would bid, and so would the Soviet, and maybe others. Anyone with that information would be sitting pretty, but it doesn't have to be a spy-ring for Russia or any other country. Oh, it might be—but let's be sure, before we start shouting Red."

"All right, old chap," Ross said.

Ross had a small flat in Bingham Mews, which lay between Regent Street and Piccadilly. He arrived there a little after one o'clock—alone. The night was still bright with stars, and he'd driven through a hushed London. He left his car outside the garage and on the other side of the mews from his flat, and stood for a few minutes, looking up at the dark window. He'd done a great deal of thinking since he had finished talking to Loftus, and it hadn't taken him very far. Now he had to wrench his mind from one kind of thought to another—he had to think about Mae.

She might be in the flat; she had a key.

He kept nothing at the flat which gave him away as a Department Z agent, so there were no fears on those grounds. But he didn't want a session with Mae tonight. If she were there she had probably watched from the window, and had seen him arrive. That needn't stop him leaving again, he could find a bed at his club.

He left the car to offer evidence that he was going out again, and approached the flight of wooden steps which led up to his front door. A gust of wind cooled his forehead as he put the key in the lock. He opened the door quietly, and stepped swiftly inside, and did not close the door again immediately. He stood still, listening for the slightest sound, any indication that Mae was here.

There was nothing.

He closed the door and went to his living-room; the door was open. He had left it open, there was nothing surprising about that. He slid his hand round the door and pressed down the switch.

The room was empty.

It was a comfortable room, and lacked nothing; he had all the money he was ever likely to want. It was oak-panelled, and there was a ledge running round the walls, with oddments standing on it; family relics, a few modest trophies, souvenirs of places and occasions abroad. The carpet was of light-brown colour, there were easy chairs, a radiogram, a piano—no bachelor could have more for his creature comfort. He didn't stay there, but went into the other rooms, taking less care. There was only one with a front window—a tiny one, which served as a dining-room; that was empty. So were his bedroom and the domestic quarters. He had a daily woman for housework, but lived here alone.

He went back into the living-room, and opened the cocktail cabinet; a nightcap and twenty minutes in an easy chair might give the night some semblance of peacefulness. He put up a hand for the whisky, and saw a letter resting on top of the bottle.

He took it down; it had no writing on the envelope.

He smiled wryly as he tore it open. There was a single sheet of his own writing-paper, and three words on it: *Dreadfully sorry—Mae.*

He poured out his drink, went to his favourite armchair and dropped in it, and read the note again. Mae had a clear, bold hand, full of character; she was full of character. Not many women would have done what she had done tonight. But what did the note mean? That she was sorry—perhaps. Why? Because she had interfered with something she now realised was important, or because she had upset him? He ought by now to be regretting some of the things he'd said, but he wasn't. The issue had been forced, and he knew that if he were compelled to choose between Mae and Department Z, Mae wouldn't win; probably she had sensed something of this. There wasn't any need to choose, they could run side by side, provided Mae gave up the fight.

Would she?

She was shrewd and clever, and she wanted him.

He didn't like it because he was able to stand outside himself and see her dispassionately; but there it was. He'd never had any illusions about Mae, but she attracted him as no other woman had ever done. He'd told himself that they would often cross swords, and would delight in the battle. He sipped again.

He sipped his drink.

At a time when he ought to be thinking of nothing but the Conway mystery, he was preoccupied with Mae, and that could hardly be worse. He ought to be thinking about Alice Conway. Just about the Professor's daughter, not her blue eyes.

The telephone bell rang.

The chair was placed so that he could take off the receiver without getting up, but he didn't stretch out his hand immediately. The bell kept ringing, and at last he picked the receiver up. It might be Mae, or it might be Craigie, and he hoped it was Craigie.

"Peter Ross speaking."

"I'm sorry to worry you so late in the evening, Mr. Ross," said a man whose voice was completely unfamiliar, "but I have a message for you."

"Thanks," said Ross, and got up slowly.

"It's signed Alice," said the man.

His voice was smooth and pleasant, and there was a ring of amusement in it—a faint hint of a chuckle, as if he could see Ross's reaction to the name of Alice. Ross tightened his grip on the telephone, and shifted his position, but his expression didn't change.

"Alice what?"

"Just Alice."

"And did she send the message through a policeman?"

"That's right, I'm a policeman."

"You'd better be careful," said Ross, "or you'll get yourself locked up."

"I'm not very worried about that," said the other mildly. "I took Alice away in a closed car, and I'm quite sure I wasn't followed—you and your friends had bigger fish to fry. Are you ready for the message?"

"Is it worth hearing?"

"I think so," said the other. "Alice says that she is quite safe and unhurt, she has been treated with great kindliness, but she's a little nervous of what might happen if the police were to find out where she is now."

"That's too bad," said Ross. "The police like to find missing girls."

"I'm sure they do. But I thought you might have a little influence with them, Mr. Ross, and suggest that it might not be in her best interests to search too far. However, that is only one of my reasons for calling you."

"I thought it might be."

"You know that if it weren't for me, Conway would be dead or out of the country, don't you?"

"It could be."

"It would be. I sent the little party at Shepperton to sleep, and I can assure you that they were most determined to take Conway away alive, or leave him behind dead and useless to anyone."

"I'll send you a bottle of Scotch with a note of thanks," said Ross dryly.

The other chuckled.

"I think if we knew each other better we should get along, Mr. Ross. At the moment I'm appealing to you as an intelligent man and a member of the Service. Don't probe too deeply yet—leave some of the investigation to me. I've served you well once, and might again—I think it would be worth your while."

"I'll think about it," said Ross.

"Do that, Mr. Ross. Good night."

The line went dead, and Ross replaced his receiver, but looked at it, scowling. Then he leaned forward and dialled the number of Craigie's office. The ringing sound started at once, and went on and on. Ross found his mind working more swiftly than before the call, found himself repeating much of what the man had said.

He had confessed to murder.

That meant that he was very sure of himself.

Craigie spoke at the other end of the line.

"It's Ross here," said Ross, and spelt his name backwards, a simple code which had served the Department well for many years. "Any news your end?"

"Nothing new, Peter. Yours?"

"I've just had an interesting call," said Ross, and explained and went on: "I don't quite make it out, but I'd say he was nervous in case we're on to him, and he thought it worth trying this way to stall us. And if he's nervous about us finding him, it means that we probably know something about him, or could find it fairly easily. That's worth thinking about."

"Did you get anything from the voice?"

"Only that I should probably recognise it again—nothing really distinctive."

"All right," said Craigie. "We'll carry on as before—if we get a line on the Conway girl we'll tell you before we do anything. Get some sleep."

Ross woke next morning with a parched mouth and a headache. He made tea, lit a cigarette, and looked through the morning newspapers. None of them carried the story of Professor Conway, which gave the Department and the police full marks. None carried any story of mysterious happenings near the river at Shepperton.

He bathed and shaved and felt better.

He breakfasted off coffee, toast, and marmalade, and by ten o'clock was talking to Loftus on the telephone; there had been no major developments. The two prisoners had been grilled, and had talked little; they had been employed by Ronald Smith, the dead tenant of the bungalows. They were bodyguards; each had a record of crime with violence. They swore they knew nothing of what had happened at the larger bungalow. They said they knew that Ronald Smith employed several other men, but knew nothing of any quarrel or break-away from Smith's gang.

Conway was still unconscious but would live. He and the three dead men had suffered from a narcotic poisoning, and the doctors had not yet decided which one; that would wait on *post mortems*.

"What about Conway's home?" Ross asked.

"He has a housekeeper who's very upset. We're doing what we can for her," said Loftus. "She's more worried about the girl than Conway—she thinks he's gone off on one of his frequent trips out of London."

"Will she tell the Press?"

"Not yet. What do you think of letting the Press know?"

"I'd hold it for a bit," said Ross.

"Right."

Loftus rang off, and Ross stood by the telephone, half-expecting it to ring, then telling himself that he was a fool. Mae would expect him to make the first move. He wouldn't be a hundred per cent on the Conway case until he'd seen her; and he wanted that hundred per cent. He worked out what he would say and how she would answer, and laughed at himself before he reached her flat.

It was in a small block near Knightsbridge, not far from Harrods. They were exclusive flats; Mae had money. She lived alone except for a middle-aged maid who had been in her family for half a century. Her family lived in the Midlands, and Ross had met them briefly.

He knew the uniformed porter on duty.

"Good morning, Mr. Ross. Nice day."

"So it is. I hadn't realised it."

"Wonderful for the time of year," said the porter, as if the weather were due to him. "Couldn't be better, could it?"

"I suppose it couldn't."

Ross went up in the lift, and at the third-floor landing started to tell himself what they would say to each other, and this time didn't laugh it off. He wasn't normal with Mae, and he couldn't stop telling himself that.

He rang the bell; there was no answer.

He had a key, but seldom used it.

He rang again, but there was no move inside the flat. That was disappointing, he didn't want to wait, wanted to get Mae and the difference with Mae completely off his mind. But it would help if he wrote a note; brief, if not so brief as hers.

He went inside, wondering idly why the maid wasn't in.

There was a wide hall, and all the doors of the flat led off it; there were only five rooms. He closed the door with a snap; all the other doors were closed. He went across to the drawing-room door, whistling softly, and thrust it open.

It was a lovely room, which looked as if it had been visited by a tornado.

Chapter 9
Second Snatch

Ross took the scene of wild disorder in at a glance, swung on his heel, and thrust open the doors of the other rooms in quick succession; they had also been visited by the tornado, the only room which had escaped was the kitchen. This was empty, but as he opened the door, he heard a dull tapping sound. He stood very still, listening; it came from the larder. He went across, and the tapping sounded louder.

He opened the door.

The maid, bound hand and foot and with a gag over her mouth, was huddled on the floor beneath the shelves. Her grey hair looked like a mop. She could just move her feet, and was tapping one against the wall. Ross drew her out gently and carried her to her room, laid her on the bed and cut the cords. As he looked at her pale, lined face, he noticed something which he'd never noticed before; her eyes were blue.

When she was free of the gag, she tried to speak and only managed to nod.

He did everything for her as he had for Alice, fighting back his own impatience. At last she could form words. He helped, by framing questions so that she had only to say yes or no, or qualify with a word or two.

This had happened before breakfast. Mae had gone for her daily before-breakfast walk, but had been due back within half an hour; she'd been gone for more than two.

There had been two men, and they had let themselves in with a key. The maid hadn't heard them come in, they'd surprised her in the kitchen, and she hadn't been able to see them clearly; all she knew was that they were young men and well dressed. They'd thrown a cloth over her face; she'd had only a swift, frightened glance at each of them.

They'd asked no questions.

Ross said: "Sure they had a key?"

"Yes—yes, Mr. Ross, there's no doubt, I'm so—so *terrified.*"

"You needn't be."

"But I am!" She was able to speak more freely now, and to move her hands without wincing. "They must have taken the key from Miss Mae's bag, where else could they have obtained it?"

"They could have stolen the bag—that's common enough."

"Then why isn't she back?" cried the maid.

Ross said: "Don't worry, I'll look after everything." He left her on the bed, knowing that the tears in her eyes were of anxiety, and went back to the drawing-room. He used the telephone, holding it with a handkerchief; there was always a chance that the men had left prints.

Craigie answered.

Ross reported.

"This is a job for the Yard," Craigie said. "They're at the bungalow, too. Stay until someone arrives, will you?"

"Who will it be?"

"Miller himself, I expect."

"Good."

"Any ideas?" asked Craigie.

Ross said: "It seems crazy, but it's connected with Conway. I think I might have an idea, too."

Craigie said: "When you've finished there, come and see me, Peter."

He rang off.

Ross surveyed the chaos. It would take hours to get the room straight, whoever had come had been looking for something small, and they had been in a fierce hurry. They'd made their own task more complicated by using tear-away methods. He couldn't guess whether they had found what they wanted, but he could guess that they'd kidnapped Mae.

Kidnapped...

He lit a cigarette, and went into Mae's bedroom. Drawers had been emptied and their contents strewn about the floor. Mae's clothes were in heaps on the floor by the wardrobe. He went across to her jewel-box.

Several rings, a pearl necklace, 'some earrings, and two diamond pendants were there.

That cut out simple robbery.

What did they think Mae had?

The telephone bell rang.

He stubbed out his cigarette and went across to it; probably this was Craigie again, with a forgotten query. He didn't even think it might be Mae, and he wasn't really surprised to hear a man.

"Mr. Ross?"

Ross said: "So it's you, is it?"

"You recognise me?" The faintly amused note was in the man's voice; a note of mockery. "I thought you would like to be reassured, Miss Harrison isn't hurt."

"You're making quite a collection," said Ross.

"Two very fine pieces," said the other, and actually chuckled. "Quite different, of course, Miss Harrison has much more spirit than Miss Conway. They're not together. They're both puzzled about my motives, though."

"Are they?"

"Aren't you?"

"They're so obvious I couldn't miss them if I were short-sighted," said Ross.

"Oh. What are they?"

Ross said: "Pressure on Conway, through his girl. Pressure on me, through Miss Harrison, plus the possibility that she had some dope on me, at the flat."

"How right!"

"Let it come," said Ross.

"I just want you to do nothing," said the man at the other end of the line. "Have a little rest. I'm sure that it will do you good, and you can be spared from your duties for a few days."

"My Boss might not agree."

The man laughed again.

"Don't be foolish, Ross. You know that you can't be forced to work on this case or any other. You can stand aside. You might be thought wise, too—you're confused because of the personal angle, aren't you? I want you to be confused, I want you to start trying to think ten ways at the same time. But most of all, I want you to take a holiday."

"And if I do?"

"The time will come when Miss Harrison will return to you, and when Miss Conway will go back home."

"I see," said Ross. "Nothing else?"

The man said: "Ross, I mean what I say. I want you off this case. If you stay on it, then I won't answer for what happens to the girls."

"One day I'll get a lot of pleasure," said Ross, "in breaking your neck."

"I'll give you twelve hours," said the other. "If you haven't withdrawn by then, I'll send you a little souvenir. You'll know that to get it, I had to cause the girls a lot of discomfort. Miss Harrison has beautiful finger-nails, hasn't she?"

Ross didn't answer.

"You sound suitably impressed."

"Oh, I'm impressed," said Ross. "Last night you were full of high ideals and good deeds, you were anxious to help. What's happened to change your mind?"

"I don't want *you* helping."

Ross said: "If you hurt either of those girls, the day will come when you won't know what hit you."

He put down the receiver.

He did not feel that he had been bright or clever; or see any way in which he could have been. He was angry; furious enough to feel the sweat on his forehead and his upper lip, to be hot when he ought to be cool. The personal worry was pressing hard; he couldn't be as dispassionate as he needed to be.

There was a ring at the front-door bell.

He answered it, to see a big man, dressed in light brown, with fair hair and a fair moustache which were turning grey. The caller looked at him from large, tired eyes. His eyelids drooped, he moved slowly as if all movement were an effort. He was Superintendent Miller of Scotland Yard.

"Good morning, Mr. Ross."

"Hallo, Super. Glad to see you."

"Everything happens at once," said Miller sorrowfully. "It's always the same. Some days we sit on our fannies and do damn-all, and the next few days we ought to be in five places at once." He turned round to look at the three Yard men who were with him. "Having a nice sleep?" he asked nastily.

The men passed, one of them smiling. One carried a small suit-case, another a camera. They went into the drawing-room, the door of which was open, and Miller followed them; he was slightly flat-footed.

"And you people always choose a day when we don't want you," complained Miller. "One bank robbery, one smash-and-grab, then there was the chap who cut his wife up into little pieces, and we haven't found all the pieces yet. And if that isn't enough…"

Ross said abruptly: "It's too much."

Miller's eyes widened; they were mild and grey.

"Have I said something I shouldn't?"

"No."

Ross went into the drawing-room, and watched one of the men opening the suit-case; it contained innumerable oddments, all the impedimenta of investigation, and he selected a bottle of grey powder and two camel-hair brushes; for finger-prints. Miller stood in the doorway and looked round.

"See that?" He pointed. "They didn't take that picture off the wall, only turned it back to front. Why didn't they make a job of it?" He sniffed. "Know what they were after?"

"No."

"No help at all," complained Miller. "It's always the same. What about the maid?"

"She's in her bedroom, and should be fit to talk by now. Not that she knows anything."

"I shouldn't expect her to," said Miller. He looked hard into Ross's set face, and then added in a quieter voice: "Don't worry, Mr. Ross, we'll find your young lady. Sims!"

He roared, and turned and hurried off, as if he were ashamed of his concession to sentiment.

Ross held out his right hand; it was quite steady, he couldn't detect any tremor. But he felt as if it were shaking. He went across the drawing-room to the picture on the wall; a painting of Mae. He'd known what it was when Miller had pointed to it, although it faced the wall. He turned it. The artist had brilliance, Mae might have been on the wall, looking down at him, with a smile which the unthinking would call inscrutable or alluring, and which was exactly the way Ross liked her best.

He turned away.

"Going?" asked Miller.

"Unless you want me?"

"No, thanks—only too glad to get on without you people hanging around and telling me how to do my job," grumbled Miller.

Ross forced a laugh, and went out.

It was warmer, and there wasn't a cloud in the sky. The porter, who looked harassed and worried because a uniformed policeman now kept him company in the hall, said that it was an even better day than yesterday, wasn't it? Ross agreed, and went to his car. The seat was hot. He drove off, but did not go immediately to Whitehall—he spent fifteen minutes driving round the side streets of London, and it helped him to make his decision. He drove to the parking-place near Whitehall, and then walked to the little door. He watched, carefully, and was quite sure that he wasn't followed.

He went in. The usual procedure was necessary, and after he had pressed his finger-nail into the slit in the rail, he waited for the door to slide open and reminded himself of what the man on the telephone had said about Mae's nails.

Craigie was alone in the office.

"Hallo, Peter. You haven't lost any time."

Ross went in, the door slid to behind him, he took out his cigarette-case and tapped a cigarette on the monogram; it was gold—a present from Mae.

"I've lost too much time," he said. "Gordon, I'm as sorry as hell about it, but I can't go on."

CHAPTER 10
OFFER REFUSED

Craigie did not answer, but led the way across the room to his desk. There was an arm-chair at each side of it. He sat down and picked up one of his meerschaums. Craigie always looked exactly the same—morning, afternoon, evening, and the middle of the night he gave the impression that he could drop off to sleep at any moment. At close quarters the myriad little lines on his forehead and round his eyes and mouth showed up. He seemed at once old and ageless. There was a droll expression at his drooping lips, and his eyes always seemed ready to smile. He carried a weight of responsibility which Ross knew was almost more than any one man could really bear. He had built up the Department from nothing; had been its leader during the last world war and the first few years of uneasy peace. He was inured to surprise, nothing really shocked him.

In this room and in others nearby there were records, many written in code; but the records were really kept in Gordon Craigie's head. He turned the still life of the written word into the vitality of the spoken one.

He sat here, day in and day out, seldom leaving the office, sifting reports from agents all over the country and all over the world. Some he passed on to associated departments; everything that had to do remotely with counterespionage in England came here. Once he had read a report, he memorised it—the trick was almost subconscious. The most remarkable thing about him was his memory. It made Loftus, his chief *aide,* give up in despair when trying to rival him. It made him the nearest thing to an indispensable man working at Whitehall—and with it all, he was mild-mannered, amiable, and filled with a deep human understanding.

"Like a drink, Peter?"

"It's too early, thanks. I'm not as bad as that."

"Mae's disappearance upset you?"

"That and the rest."

"Anything I don't know about?"

"Nothing you can't guess," said Ross, and laughed. "Gordon, I'm no more use to you."

"What makes you think so?"

"Until this job, I could put everything else out of my mind. It was like closing a door. This was the work I wanted to do and was doing, and everything else was outside it— fun and games. I know why you used to bar married men, and why you wish you still could. Since last night I've been doodling like a callow youth in love for the first time. I even get my women mixed up!"

He paused.

"Go on," said Craigie.

"Look at it this way. My job is to keep Conway free of trouble, and to find out who's getting at him and this air-defence business. Well, I've had jobs as sticky. They've been the beginning and the end of existence. Oh, I've had fun between and taken an easy spell or so, and hit the tiles pretty hard. The objective has been as clear as the sun on a warm June day—sorry if I sound like a sentimental rhymester! This time, I can't see the objective properly. It's hiding behind something—someone—else. I'll go a long way to find Mae and as far to find Alice Conway, but *not* because it's part of the job. They're objectives in themselves. I'm going to run into trouble in that frame of mind, and you know it."

Craigie was fiddling with his meerschaum.

"Isn't that enough?" asked Ross abruptly.

"No." Craigie smiled, and his eyes twinkled.

Ross laughed, shortly.

"What do you use for eyes? X-ray lenses? All right, there's something else. The mysterious merchant telephoned me again this morning—with orders. I am to take a holiday, and leave everything to you. No, he didn't mention you by name, but told me to clear out and leave it to others. He added that if I didn't, I'd get a souvenir. One of Mae's finger-nails, or such like." Ross's voice was brittle. "Now, stop me thinking more about Mae, if you can."

"I don't know that I want to. Find Mae, and you've probably found this man."

"Try to find him and fail, and what will happen to Mae and the other girl?"

Craigie seemed satisfied with the big pipe, and lit it. His calm should have been irritating, but Ross found it oddly soothing. Craigie wasn't amused, impatient, or intolerant, he gave the impression that he knew all the different tensions in the other's mind.

"Listen, Peter. I don't think I've a man on the books who hasn't handed in his resignation, sooner or later. Most of them make it pretty soon—you've lasted a long time. Even Bill Loftus…"

"No!"

Craigie smiled. "Loftus ran into a packet rather worse than yours. His wife—his first wife—was killed. It knocked him to pieces, and he didn't think he'd ever be any good at the game again. But he held on by the skin of his teeth, and the Department would be in a poor way without him. There are others, by the dozen. Men you know, men you'd think had never known a moment's weakness, once nearly cracked. This job demands something more than the ordinary human being can stand. You have to be slightly inhuman to get through; you have to reject the ordinary human emotions and passions part of the time, and when the clash comes— and it's bound to come—the human-being side comes on top first. Usually, the other side soon gets restive. For instance, if you were to throw your hand in, and do what Mr. X wanted— what do you think you'd be feeling this time next week?"

Ross didn't answer.

"You're probably thinking that provided Mae and Alice were all right, you'd be glad you'd washed your hands of it. Well, you wouldn't. And every time you looked at Mae, you'd have a sinking feeling inside you, and you'd wonder why you didn't feel as you used to. For your own sake I'd say—don't be an ass, carry on."

Ross said: "Well, supposing you stop thinking about me, and think of the Department."

Craigie said: "I see."

He opened one of the drawers in his desk and took out a book. It was a slim volume, in black covers, about six inches by eight. He opened it and scanned one or two pages; even upside down, Ross saw that the writing was Craigie's, neat and impeccable. Craigie smoothed his forehead and turned the book round, pushing it towards Ross.

"See that?"

There were names and brief biographies. The last entry was at the foot of the page, and the ink on it was paler than most of the others. It read:

Henry Michael (Harry) Marshall. Born 1916. Married. One daughter, Sarah. Entered Department's service July 1943. Died in Department's service May 195...

By the side of the entry was a number '117'.

Ross closed the book and handed it back.

"With a few exceptions, it takes years to train an agent," said Craigie. "Even when he's been vetted and passed into service, he has years of donkey work to do, and only one in four get right past the stage after which he can take charge of missions. One in ten, maybe, is outstanding. Loftus is the one you know best, but you've met several of the others. The casualty rate is shockingly high—since I started that register, I've had three hundred and nine different agents, and, apart from the fatal casualties, at least fifty aren't fit for the job any more. That's how it is, Peter. When a man reaches your stage in the Department, I want to keep him. I know there's a risk—you might be the exception who would really fall down because of Mae, but I don't think so. I think you'd find that you could put the Department first—and without being naïve, remember that means the country—and the rest second. And once you've managed that, you'd be all right."

Ross didn't speak.

Craigie went on mildly: "When the clash between the agent and the man comes for the first time, it makes hell for them both. After that things settle down. You're two people—sometimes the agent, sometimes the man, and the two don't mix easily."

"I see," said Ross, heavily.

"It's up to you," said Craigie. "You know yourself better than I do, if you're sure that you ought to back down—no one will blame you. Certainly Bill Loftus and I shan't. We'll be sorry, but we'll find someone else. Loftus might take it on himself."

"No one else available?" Ross asked abruptly.

"Not without taking them off another job."

"Well, I've warned you."

Craigie smiled again.

"We cover everyone we can, you might fail, and if you do someone will have to take over. You could fail because of the human element, or you could simply be shot or be run over—replacement would be necessary in either case, and I'd have the job of finding the replacement."

"I see," said Ross, abruptly. "And how often do you feel like telling bumptious little squirts like me where to get off?"

Craigie chuckled.

"We haven't much to go on," Craigie said a few minutes afterwards, "but we do know that Mr. X is very anxious to have you out of the game. That means that he knows you've something on him…"

"I haven't a clue."

"…which you don't realise," Craigie went on as if there had been no interruption. "Or else he judged from what happened last night, and thinks you'll probably cause him a lot of trouble. There's one odd thing…"

"I know," said Ross. "Why make a set at me, when the normal reaction would be to make me get more stubborn and jump into the case with both feet."

"Could he know that Mae wants to keep you out?"

"Someone who knew about the row," murmured Ross, and his eyes sparkled. "I haven't told the world. Mae certainly wouldn't. Leaving you, Bill, and one or two others from the Department out, what do we have?"

"Everyone who was at the Dive last night," said Craigie.

Ross jumped up.

"Eye-witnesses to the ring's return trip—there weren't more than thirty. Half of them I know by name, and Sam will know the rest. I'm on my way, Gordon."

Chapter 11
Sam

The Dive had a reputation for being spiced with danger, moderately illegal, and consequently mildly risky. In fact, it was as respectable a bar as could be found in London. The causes for its fashionable success were as puzzling as the causes of women's fashions. It had been opened by a prize-fighter who had retired from the ring, bought by an ex-naval commander, passed on to a syndicate, sold out to a peer of the realm; and it had neither flourished nor failed spectacularly. Finally, a mild-mannered, husky-voiced Lancastrian, who was warned that he was buying a white elephant because all the wide boys of London would fleece him, had bought the place at a modest price.

According to the owner, Higson, on his first day of business a soft-voiced ebony streak, whose name was Ebenezer Theodore Wilson White, had sidled through the doorway, wormed his way into the nearly empty bar, wriggled through the narrow door behind the bar which led to the owner's office; there, grinning with nervousness, twisting and rubbing his black hands, and scraping one foot against the other, he had stood in front of the Lancastrian.

He was known to be a Jamaican who had been a steward on many steamship lines, knew the world, and liked

London. Apparently he had been out of work and was broke. Higson had often said that all he remembered of that first interview was white teeth, big eyes which rolled and a mop of frizzy black hair—and Sam's voice. Higson also said that but for that rich, deep yet soft voice, and the way in which Ebenezer Theodore Wilson White had uttered each syllable with husky relish, he would not have given him a job.

A Canadian, the first to drink one of the new barman's *Dive Specials,* had called him Sam.

Now he was Sam to hundreds.

It was twenty past eleven—and the first customers at the Dive could be expected soon after eleven-thirty—when Ross reached the bar. Sam was behind the polished counter, giving a little extra polish to glasses. He was immaculate in a starched white coat and black trousers, wore a winged collar and a black bow, and as Ross entered he dropped a glass. He grabbed at it wildly, backed, made the many-coloured bottles on the shelves ring, and finally lifted the unbroken glass high, in excited triumph.

"Good morning to yo', sah. I'm mighty glad to see yo' so early. Get's kinda lonesome before opening time, yessah. Yo' all that thirsty, Massa Ross?"

"It's too early to be thirsty."

"Sho' t'ing, if yo' intend to be legal," agreed Sam. "I kinda can't understand the laws in this country, Massa Ross. Human beings ain't made fo' laws, that's my opinion. No, sah. It's ridiculous, Massa Ross, at one minute to opening time yo' ain't thirsty, and at one minute after—oh, boy, yo' so thirsty yo' can drink just as much as yo' like. Ain't I right, Massa Ross?"

"Not far out, Sam."

"What's it going to be, Massa Ross?"

"A pink gin, on the stroke of eleven-thirty."

"Sure t'ing, on the very stroke of eleven-thirty," said Sam, and held up his huge hand to display an R.A.F. wristwatch with great pride. He contrived to prise the top of the watch from his wrist and turn the hands gradually, peering at it with his eyes nearly popping out of his head. "See that, Massa Ross? Half past eleven exactly! Yo' said pink gin?"

"Pink gin, Sam."

Sam turned and did conjuring tricks with bottles and a glass. His face was set and serious, lips pursed, and Ross saw all that in the big mirror behind the bar.

"Sam."

"Yes, sah?"

"Do you remember anything unusual happening here last night?"

"Who, sah? Me, sah? No, sah!"

"Sam."

Sam turned, slowly, and with a flourish put the drink down on the counter.

"Pink gin, sah."

"You wouldn't lie to me, would you, Sam?" Ross pushed a pound note across the desk, and Sam flicked it towards the till and rang three shillings. He busied himself with change.

"No, sah, I wouldn't lie to you or any other gennulmen. I didn't notice anything unusual in this place last night; how should I know if it's unusual, Massa Ross? I don't understand what yo' want me to say I saw if I didn't see nothin'."

"Sam."

Sam's face was like ebony after rain.

"It ain't none of my business, Massa Ross, if some of my clients hab diff'rences of opinion; yo' must admit that's the solemn truth. Yes, sah, I don't have eyes where my eyes didn't ought to be; I got better use for my eyes than anything like that, Massa Ross. If anyone was to ask me, I wouldn't even be sure yo' and the lady were here last night, no, sah. Seventeen shillings change, Massa Ross."

"It's yours, Sam."

"You're mighty kind, Massa Ross. I'm telling yo' I clean forgot you and the lady was in this Dive." Sam beamed with enormous relief. "Yo' don't need to worry, Massa Ross, and I'm ashamed of yo'. Yes, sah, I'm ashamed of yo', thinking that I would tell anyone that I'd seen something I couldn't have seen because I wasn't looking. I wasn't even sure that yo' were in the Dive, Massa Ross!"

"Anyone else been asking you questions, Sam?"

"No, sah!"

"You've a wonderful memory."

"Yes, sah! There can't be a better memory in London if I saw a thing, but I couldn't remember a thing I couldn't see, Massa Ross. Don't you worry. How is the lady?"

"She's fine. Did you see her when she left?"

Sam shifted his feet, noisily, and corrected the position of his tie, enabling it to dodge his Adam's apple.

"Sho', seeing it's you that's asking me, sah."

"Did you see everyone else in the Dive?"

Sam's forehead wrinkled into black corrugated iron, and his eyes darted to and fro. There was no sound on the staircase, nothing to suggest that anyone else was near, although he gave the impression that he was looking for salvation, having no love for this conversation.

Then he beamed, as if suddenly delighted with the world.

"Massa Ross, I don't properly understand yo', no sah. I always told myself and Massa Higson, true as I'm here, I always told the two of us that there wasn't a nicer gennulman than Massa Ross, anywhere in the world, and I've travelled all over the world, Massa Ross, and I've always told——"

"Were there any strangers here, Sam?"

Sam stopped talking, his forehead smoothed out, he looked about ten years old.

"Yo' mean, did I see anyone I didn't know before?"

"Yes."

"No, sah, they was all old clients. I don't understand yo', Massa Ross."

"Sure you recognised them all?"

"Certain sho'."

"Could you name them?"

Sam licked his lips and leaned on the bar.

"Why don't yo' ask what you want to ask, Massa Ross? I wouldn't hold out on a gentleman like yo'."

"Did you find anything here, after I'd left?"

"Find?' echoed Sam, in a ruminative fashion. "No, sah, I didn't find anything. You lost something?"

"Yes."

"I'm mighty sorry 'bout that. What was it, Massa Ross?"

"I just lost something."

"Well, I didn't find nothin'."

"Then someone else did, Sam, and I want to know who was here, because if I know who was here I can tell who found this thing."

"Sho'," said Sam, in a hushed whisper. "Sho' yo' could. I'm not so dumb I can't understand a simple thing like that."

Ross took out a slip of paper; there were nineteen names on it. He turned it round so that Sam could see, and Sam's eyes, nearly popping out of his head, concentrated on that list. It was now really twelve o'clock, but no one else had come in. Sam's pink tongue ran along his lips, and he took a propelling-pencil from the pocket of his stiff white coat and added two more names, then licked the pencil and stared up at the ceiling and almost immediately added another three. Then he looked round the room, staring at each table and set of chairs in turn, as if making a mental calculation. He added more names, at intervals, then counted the number of the list and did more counting on his fingers; they moved with ridiculous ease and speed.

He finished.

"That's the whole lot, Massa Ross."

Ross didn't say "Are you sure?" but took the list. Sam had an upright schoolboyish writing, but it was legible; and Ross remembered three of the people he'd noted down as having been at the Dive when he had quarrelled with Mae. He folded the list and put it in his pocket.

"Have a drink with me, Sam?"

"You're mighty kind, Massa Ross. I don't mind if I do, sah."

"And another pink gin for me."

"Sho'."

"Any of these people who don't come often, Sam?"

"They come and they don't come, if you see what I mean, boss."

"Any of them been here with Miss Harrison?"

Sam closed his eyes and wrinkled his forehead again, exuded a long, slow breath, mixed the drink, slapped them on the counter, and said:

"Not lately, sah."

"How long ago?"

" 'Fore you came along, Massa Ross, maybe t'ree, maybe four months ago."

"Who was it?"

"Why, Mr. Barnard, sah."

Ross had a quick mental picture of James Barnard, tall, sleek, wealthy, who had been a friend of Mae's; not her only friend by a long way.

"Anyone else?"

"No, sah."

"Sam, you've been wonderful, and you have the best memory in the world, remember?"

"You got me dead right, Massa Ross!"

"Can you remember any of these people who were *always* around when I was here with Miss Harrison, and who came in after us and left soon after, too?"

"Massa Ross," said Sam feelingly, "yo' sho' do ask the most diff'cult questions. Now lemme see. You and Miss Harrison come in, and then this guy comes in and you goes out and he goes out. That right?"

"Exactly right, Sam."

"Last night?"

"Last night and any night."

Sam said: "I—I dunno, sah."

Ross sighed.

"Now try hard."

He read the first name on the list, aloud. Sam looked blank. The second and third—a man named Bray.

Sam hesitated.

"Bray, now," said Ross. "What did he do last night?"

"Massa Bray, sah, he looked mighty pleased after yo' had gone, I don't see why I shouldn't tell yo' that a gentleman looked so pleased he grinned all over his face. He was kind of looking down, and if you remember, Massa Ross, he was in the corner." Sam pointed to an empty space, and stabbed his finger towards another. "You and Miss Harrison was *there*, sah, and Mr. Bray, he was *there*. You and Miss Harrison had yo' little misunderstanding, but Massa Bray was very busy, I guess he wouldn't notice. He was with a lady, sah—and then when you'd gone, I guess he wasn't long after yo'. The lady, she went with him, and Massa Bray was *mighty* pleased. I guess he an' the lady had come to an understanding."

"Possibly, Sam," said Ross. Ross read out the other names, but Sam was vague. He finished and narrowed one eye. "You've a very bad memory, haven't you?"

Sam gaped.

"You don't remember me asking any of these questions, do you?"

Sam grinned, and his face was like a mirror.

"You beat dem all, Massa Ross, yo' sho' do. Yaash, sah, I got the worstest mem'ry in all of London. He-he-he!" Sam slapped the counter and then his side, and doubled up with merriment and was all teeth. "I just don't recall a word you've said, Massa Ross, not a word, not now or any other time."

"Wonderful, Sam! Oh, Mr. Bray was with Dolly Leeming, wasn't he?"

"That's right, sah." Sam looked troubled.

"Thanks."

Ross winked, finished his drink, and went to the cloak-room. Light voices sounded on the stairs as the door swung to; and three minutes afterwards, when he went back, eight people were in front of Sam, and others were coming in; the Dive was beginning to wake up. He went out, casting a swift glance at the telephone, decided that he would call Craigie from his flat, and drove there, fast.

He was thinking of Sammy Bray, a man known to hundreds of the Mayfair and the Dive set, short, chubby, genial, everyone's friend, every girl's uncle, a man with a hundred fingers and each one in a pie. He didn't know why he felt so sure that Bray was the man he was after; there was a lot to do before he could be sure.

He opened the front door and stepped inside.

A man behind the door smashed a cosh at his head.

Chapter 12
Attack

Ross glimpsed the arm, hand, and cosh as he was moving, flung himself forward and felt the weapon sharply on the back of his head; painful but not deadly. He swivelled round on one foot, with the other leg stretched out, and cracked his toe-cap against the assailant's knee.

The man, short, lean, unshaven, was striking at him again. Ross got home first, the second blow of the cosh just brushed his shoulder. He went like a bullet at his assailant next, pummelling face and stomach, driving the man back to the wall. The cosh dropped with a heavy thud, the man began to moan in protest and surrender.

Ross dropped his arms and stood back.

"Good morning," he said.

The man leaned against the wall, arms by his sides, mouth open, blood smearing his lips and chin and spotting his white shirt. He had greying hair and a pot-belly, the top button of the trousers wouldn't do up.

"Tired?" asked Ross.

The man gulped in an effort to speak, but couldn't make it. Ross moved forward, and the other cringed back, but all Ross did was to dip inside his coat pocket and bring out a tattered wallet and two envelopes, and to pat his other pockets, to make sure he hadn't another weapon. Then Ross bent down and picked up the cosh. It was black and smooth, about a foot long, thicker at one end than the other. He felt it, and the lead shot with which the head was packed moved sluggishly under the pressure. He swung it through the air, and it made a hissing sound—and also made its owner cringe away again.

"So you only want to hand it out," said Ross. He moved away, tossed the cosh on to a hall chair, and looked through the wallet. He didn't expect to find much, and wasn't pleasantly surprised. There was a registration card and a few other oddments, but nothing which was likely to give Ross much information—except the man's name and address. According to the registration card, he was Herbert William Cary. The two letters were addressed to H. Cary in an almost illiterate scrawl; he did not think that he would learn much from the letters, but slipped them into his pocket with the wallet—and smiled. He felt more at ease now than he had since he had first started out for Shepperton; this encounter had done him good. So had the fact that although he'd walked into it, blind as a bat, he hadn't lost a moment. No one could complain about the way he'd reacted; he didn't even want to complain to himself.

"And do they call you Bert or Bill?" he asked.

Cary licked his lips.

"Thirsty?" asked Ross. "Come and have a drink."

He turned his back on the man and thrust open the door of the living-room. He expected Cary to make a rush for the front door, but Cary seemed dazed, and meekly followed him, shuffling his feet. He wore long, pointed shoes, a light-brown reefer suit which needed cleaning and was frayed at the cuffs, a soiled white shirt, and a tie with so many colours that it had to be seen to be believed. He also wanted a haircut and a shave. He shuffled into the living-room, while Ross held the door open for him and made a mock bow.

"Do sit down," said Ross.

The man obeyed, dropping into an arm-chair and making a spring groan.

"Whisky?" asked Ross.

Cary looked at him from bloodshot eyes, as if he were sure he would wake up in a moment, and then the nightmare would really begin. This wasn't real, to him. He gaped as Ross went to the cabinet and took out the whisky.

"Soda?"

Cary gulped.

"Sure—sure."

Ross was sparing with the soda, and pushed the glass into Cary's unsteady hand. Cary stared at him, at the drink, and then gulped it down as if he were afraid that it might be snatched away from him. Ross watched this performance, smiling mildly, one hand in his pocket. Cary put the glass down on a handy table, and drew in his feet.

"You'll feel more talkative after that," said Ross. "Who sent you here, Bert?"

"I..."

"Go on," said Ross encouragingly. "Who sent you? A mysterious man you've never seen except in the dark, whom you always meet by appointment, and whose name you don't know."

"Lumme!" breathed Cary. "How did you guess?"

"Oh, it always happens that way," said Ross airily. "I've come across it a dozen times, and haven't you read it in books? Perhaps you don't read books. They're as good as racing form, Bert, and would do you much more good. Who sent you?"

"I—I don't know, he..."

"Now listen," said Ross, "we've had the fun. You hit me over the head, and I hit you back, and then to make up the difference in ages, I gave you a drink. That makes us square—no offence taken, none intended. But I want to know who sent you."

Cary averted his gaze and didn't answer.

Ross said: "Look," in a very gentle voice.

Cary glanced up—and found the muzzle of an automatic only a yard from his face. He reared back, putting up his hands as if they would fend off bullets. He had a thin face with a button of a nose, and his ears stuck out.

"Supposing we don't argue. Who sent you?"

Cary muttered: "Tiger."

"Oh, really."

"I—I tell you it was Tiger, but if he finds out…"

"Tiger who?"

"Just—Tiger."

"Oh," said Ross, and wondered if by chance there was a man in London whose surname was Tiger. "What did he tell you to do?"

"I—I had to open your tin."

"Oh," said Ross, puzzled. "Sardine tin?"

"Tin, can, *safe,*" muttered Cary. "That's what I had to do, but if Tiger finds out I've told you…"

"What were you to take from my safe?"

"Everything!"

"Well, well," said Ross, "he's a pretty hopeful chap, this Tiger. Nothing special?"

"No!"

"Were you to look anywhere else?"

"Just the safe," said Cary.

"Now I wonder what particular thing Tiger wanted," said Ross and looked down into the barrel of the automatic.

"Nasty things these, aren't they, and I'm told it's legal to shoot a house-breaker caught red-handed and threatening violence."

"Mister, you wouldn't…"

"You'd be surprised what I would do if I'm roused," said Ross. "What were you looking for at Mae Harrison's flat this morning?"

If Cary had pleaded for the next twenty-four hours that he had never heard of Mae Harrison, his expression would have given him away. He didn't answer to the maid's description very well, but there was no doubt that he had searched Mae's flat. He stared at the gun, which was now levelled towards him, as if afraid that it might go off at any moment. His long hands clutched the arms of his chair, his lips were parted, and his tongue kept darting out, running along his lips from one corner to the other and then disappearing again. He was breathing heavily; that was the only sound in the flat.

"Well, what did you want from that flat?" asked Ross.

"I don't know."

"I see—you just have to close your eyes and wish, and you'd be inspired to know what Tiger wanted."

"I only had to do the job, I didn't have to look for anything, I had a cove with me."

"Tiger?"

"No," said Cary, and as nearly as he could, while feeling so scared, he sounded derisive. "Just a pal to keep a look-aht. 'E couldn't come this time."

"Your bad luck. Sure it wasn't Tiger?"

"Tiger never does the job hisself, you ought to know that."

"Don't blame me, blame my father," said Ross, "he must have neglected my education. So you had someone with you when you went to Miss Harrison's flat, and he knew what he was after, but didn't tell you."

"Tha's right!"

Ross said softly: "You're a liar. What did you go for?"

Cary muttered: "Tiger just told me to look rahnd, take what I could put me 'ands on. Anyfink."

That could be true. But why?

"How did you get in?" Ross asked.

"He had a key."

"And here?"

"Tiger give me a key. That's the truth, he give me one!" Cary wriggled to one side and dived his hand into his pocket, then drew out a Yale key and held it aloft, triumphant. "See!"

"And he didn't tell you where he got it?"

"Of course he didn't," said Cary, witheringly. "Tiger never tells you anything. Mister, I didn't do you no 'arm, I wouldn't 'ave——"

"They ought to have christened you George Washington," said Ross, mildly. "Ever met Miss Harrison?"

"Who?"

"Never mind. Where did you meet this man who was at the flat with you?"

" 'E come wiv me."

"Did Tiger know?"

"No—just give me the job."

"Where does Tiger live?"

Cary said: "If you don't know, you can find out easy enough. Mister, I didn't want to do the job, but I got a wife and kids, I gotta live, they..."

"I seem to have heard that one before somewhere," said Ross. "It won't work, Cary."

He glanced away from the prisoner towards the safe, which was in a corner, hidden by a small, built-in cupboard.

The door was open, but the contents were still there. Most of the contents would have been no use to any burglar; there were deeds of properties, his will, a few share certificates, a few trifles of jewellery, watches, two more cigarette-cases. There was nothing about the Department there, and that was the only thing he could imagine Cary's employer wanted.

"Where does Tiger live?" he asked, turning slowly.

"Cor' strewth, why arst me? Whitechapel, *everyone* knows Tiger. Mister, I never did you no 'arm, did I? I 'aven't busted the safe, you can lock it again, it's only an old one—why, any kid could open a can like that. You don't 'ave to..."

"I ought to, you need a few months in the cooler, Bert. I've your name and address and can put the police on to you in five minutes. You know that."

Cary didn't speak.

"Go into the kitchen and wait there," said Ross.

Cary got up slowly, looking as if he thought this was also a trick, and sidled towards the door. Ross grinned as he watched the man glance at the front door, and then turn towards the kitchen; he knew the way, which meant that he had looked through the flat before starting work on the safe. Ross closed the door with a bang, and then went to the telephone and dialled Craigie's number. He watched the door all the time, but there was no sound and no sign of movement.

Craigie answered.

"There's a little man, forty-ish, five-feet six, light-brown suit, greying hair, pot-bellied, and with pointed shoes and a tie that is a lineal descendent of Joseph's coat," said Ross.

"Where?" asked Craigie.

Ross chuckled.

"In my kitchen. I'm going to let him go in a few minutes. How long will it take you to have someone here to follow him?"

"Twenty minutes," said Craigie.

"Will you fix it?" asked Ross. "I'll hold on, I've one or two other things."

"Yes."

Craigie went off, and next moment Ross heard his voice as he spoke into another telephone. Ross watched the door, half-expecting Cary to be outside, turning the handle or trying to listen at the keyhole.

Craigie was soon back.

"What's the rest, Peter?"

"There's a Samuel Bray, plumpish and all merry and bright, one of the new socialites who's often at the Dive," said Ross. "I think he'll be worth checking. Nothing definite, but he took unholy joy in my row with Mae last night. His latest girl friend is Dolly Leeming, *ex* front row of the chorus. Ten years *ex*. She was with Bray last night. And then there's a sleek, smooth type, named James Barnard, who used to know Mae well and who's an outsider. Can you vet them all?"

"Yes."

"Thanks," said Ross. "And have you ever heard of a man named Tiger?"

"Willy Tiger?"

Ross gulped.

"I didn't ask his pet name. He lives in Whitechapel."

"That's right, Seventeen Millicent Street," said Craigie promptly—and chuckled. "I think you might enjoy meeting the Tiger. Thinking of trying to?"

"What's the snag?" asked Ross suspiciously.

"He's just…" said Craigie, and broke off. "Sorry, it's not important, I've a caller." He rang off, leaving Ross holding the receiver with one hand and smoothing the back of his head gingerly with the other. Ross shrugged and put the receiver down. He glanced at his watch; it was five minutes to one. He went to the door silently, and pulled it open abruptly.

Cary wasn't there.

Cary was sitting on the kitchen draining-board, looking thoroughly miserable.

He sprang up.

"Can I go?"

"Not as soon as all that," said Ross. "Cut me some sandwiches, there's a chunk of meat in the larder, and make me some coffee. Open a small tin of fruit, and lay that tray—for one, I'm not giving free meals. Then you can scram."

He went out again, sat back in his living-room, eyes closed, head aching slightly, very preoccupied about a man named Willy Tiger.

Cary brought in the tray; a Savoy waiter couldn't have done a better job.

"Now clear out," said Ross.

Cary didn't waste any time saying thanks, just streaked for the door, casting one swift look back, as if he expected the gun to pop out of Ross's pocket again. As a precaution he slammed the door. Ross heard him running down the steps and across the mews, but didn't get up. If he'd troubled to do that, he would have seen the wiry Perry following the little crook.

Ross ate leisurely and thought still more about Willy Tiger. Craigie didn't rate him high, but Cary did; and Cary's employers were Mae's kidnappers; they were using Tiger, and that suggested that they also rated him fairly high. Was it possible that Craigie had made a mistake? It was possible, but not likely.

Ross could get more information, Miller and others at the Yard would be free with it, but that would prejudice him. He wanted to meet Willy Tiger and form his own opinions.

He left the flat at five past two.

Chapter 13
Tiger

Whitechapel was noisy and crowded. Cars hummed, lorries roared, two-decker buses grumbled, and cyclists thronged the sides of the roads. Outside nearly every shop a man or woman stood waiting hopefully for custom and talking persuasively to anyone who dawdled nearby. A sergeant and a policeman stood on a corner, watching the flowing traffic and the hurrying people with an almost regal air. Now and again a flashily dressed girl passed; as often, a youth with broad, squared shoulders and a suit which looked too big for him; without exception, these wore ties which competed with Cary's. Barrow-boys pushed their barrows and cried their wares, fruit on the barrows looked bright and appetising. An old woman sat in front of a huge flower-stall on the corner opposite the policeman, and seemed to be nodding herself to sleep.

Ross drew alongside the policeman. The sergeant leaned towards his car.

"Can I help you, sir?"

"I'm looking for Millicent Street."

"Oh," said the sergeant, a large man, and paused, as if to take in the gleaming car and the well-dressed driver. "Any special part of it?"

"Just Millicent Street, I'm told it's nearby."

"Yes, sir." A large forefinger pointed. "Third on the right and then second left, that's it, sir. The Mission is right at the other end."

"Oh, thanks," said Ross, and smiled as if his only interest was the Mission.

He nodded and slid into the stream of traffic.

The second turning on the left was past the shell of the big church and the clock-tower of the library. He slid round the corner, out of the hustle and din of this hub of the East End, into drab quiet. The road was long, narrow and dingy. Small terrace houses with front door opening on to the pavement were on either side. Near the corner a woman stood against a doorway, a baby at her breast, while another, much older, talked to her in a whining undertone. Several children, all tiny, all looking much healthier than the women, were running along the pavement with a muted eagerness which hardly seemed natural. A youth leaned against a lamp-post, reading a newspaper—*The Sporting Times*. As Ross passed, the youth glanced at him over the top of the page, and followed him as he drove slowly towards the far end. He had to go slowly; there were more children, and they darted into the roadway without warning, without caring that he was there. A young girl waved to him; the sun glistened on her lipstick and made the only touch of brightness here.

The road curved.

As Ross reached the middle of the curve, he saw two larger buildings, nearly opposite each other. Each had a big placard, and that on the right read:

GARAGE

YOU CAN BE SURE OF

SHELL

The garage consisted of a large tin shed. Outside it were several bicycles, two motor cycles, and three cars, two very old and dilapidated, the other glistening and modern—a streamlined Morris.

The sign on the left read:
CRUSADE FOR YOUTH
MISSION
H.Q.

The Mission House was a shed as large as the garage, and was actually farther along the road. There was nothing outside except a small sports car, parked near the kerb. The front of the Mission shed was of wood, and had been freshly painted; several placards outside it offered a pithy challenge to passers-by. The two buildings seemed to vie with each other, and for attractiveness, the Mission House had it.

The house next to the garage was Number 15. So the garage was Number 17.

As Ross pulled up, eyes appeared at nearby windows, and a youth with long hair, an oily face, and a pair of patched dungarees slouched from the garage doorway towards the solitary petrol-pump.

" 'Ow much?"

"Hallo," said Ross, and climbed out.

He nodded and walked past the youth. The shed was huge; several cars stood about in various stages of repair, and three mechanics were working; they seemed to be working hard. A lathe was running at the back of the shed, and sparks came off a piece of metal which was being buffed. No one took any notice of Ross. At the far end was a large window, very dirty, but admitting some light, and in a corner near it was a wooden partition, on the door of which was the legend: Office.

The youth drifted up.

"Want someone?"

"Is Tiger in?"

" 'E's busy."

"Pity," said Ross.

He went towards the door, and a hand clutched his sleeve. The oily-faced youth looked at him in alarm; no other word could describe it.

"I told yer, 'e's busy."

"Not too busy to see me," said Ross.

The youth let him go. The expression in the bright eyes was one of wariness, warning, and cynical amusement; he couldn't have said "You've asked for it" any more clearly. Ross reached the door, and heard voices. There was no window in the office, it was impossible to see what was happening inside. He didn't tap, but pulled the door open.

A man said in a raucous voice:

"That's it and all abaht it, you clear aht. I don't want you arahnd. *Get to 'ell aht of it!*" the man went on in a vicious tone, and glared at Ross.

Ross didn't move, but slid his right hand into his coat pocket.

The man sitting at a small, littered desk was in his shirt-sleeves, and the neck of the shirt was open to show the top of a hairy chest and a dirty singlet with a blue trimming. He had a huge neck, a small head, and big, tawny brown eyes. He hadn't shaved for days. There was strength and power in his body, in the great arms resting on the desk, in his enormous hands. His eyes were huge, and their unusual colour made them remarkable. He had a broad nose, a big chin, and a wide mouth, and the lower lip was thrust forward so that the two sabre teeth showed, white and pointed. No one could have lived up to his name more than Willy Tiger.

He spoke from the back of his throat in a guttural roar.

"You 'eard me—get to 'ell aht of it!"

"Good afternoon," said Ross, and went farther in.

He looked at the second man, who was standing up; a youngish, clean-cut man, red-haired, fresh-faced—and flushed. He wore a clerical collar and a suit of clerical grey.

"Listen!" growled Willy Tiger, "I'm a patient man, I am. I can stand a lot of trouble, but I just don't want to see more of you—neiver of you. Just do me a favour and scram. Vamoose. Skedaddle."

"But there's so much I want to say to you, Tiger," said Ross.

"Reely." Tiger breathed through distended nostrils. "So you got a lot to say, like this slab-sided son of a…"

"Be quiet, Willy," said Ross, and drowned the last word.

His voice blared out much louder than Tiger's, startling the man into silence.

The clergyman said: "It's hopeless, the man's a menace to the whole district. Tiger, if you take any more of my boys away, I'll find a way of dealing with you. I've tried persuasion, but you won't listen to reason. In future you'll run into a lot of trouble."

He turned away.

"Trouble! Me! Why, you ginger-haired baboon, what do you think you're doing? Threatening *me.*" Tiger jumped to his feet, and Ross was startled; he wasn't much more than five feet tall, but vast across the chest and shoulders. He shook his huge fist and rounded the desk, looked as if he would hurl himself at the clergyman. "Don't you come into me garrich agine, understand, or I'll throw you aht. You needn't think you can 'ide behind no dog collar wiv me, *I* don't pay any attention to your smooth talk. Don't give me any threats, mister, or I'll…"

He grabbed the clergyman's wrist.

Ross said: "Steady, or..."

And then he moved back, for the clergyman drove his free fist hard into Tiger's stomach, brought an ouch of pain and astonishment, wrenched his right hand free and clipped Tiger on the jaw. Tiger, completely unprepared for such tactics, swayed back, hit against the desk and sent a bottle of ink to the floor. Blue ink splashed and then spread in a widening pool.

"Why—why, you..." breathed Tiger, and drew himself up, then bounded forward.

He had long arms, brushed the clergyman's right arm aside, and drove a blow at his stomach. He didn't get home. The clergyman pushed his arm away and let go with a straight left which smashed into Tiger's mouth, sending Tiger reeling back.

He said softly: "I've warned you, Tiger."

Before Tiger could recover or speak, while he was still tasting the salt blood at his lips, the clergyman swung out of the office. The youth and two others had been gaping spectators of the fight, and backed away as if afraid that the battling cleric would start on them. He strode across the garage and went out like a storm.

Tiger straightened up, and put a hand to his mouth. He took it away, and stared dazedly at the blood.

"Why," he muttered, "I'll tear 'im apart. I'll tear 'im into little pieces and feed 'im to the dogs."

Ross murmured: "You started it."

Tiger gulped and blinked, and turned towards him. The tawny eyes were bloodshot, but that wasn't the worst. Ross had seen hatred and evil in men's eyes, but none more naked nor more livid than his. Tiger was more animal than human. He drew in a shuddering breath, and clenched his fists, and his voice seemed to come from a long way off.

"I told you to clear aht, mister. You 'eard me."

"But I want a little talk, Tiger."

Tiger licked his lips, which were bleeding more freely now, and his rage didn't fade. He lashed out suddenly in a two-fisted attack, but Ross backed, grabbed one of the wrists and twisted. Tiger opened his mouth and gave a startled squeal; he stopped moving, for his arm was forced into a position from which he knew he couldn't escape without breaking bones. Ross stood beaming at him.

The spectators gasped.

Ross let Tiger go, backed, and closed the door with his foot. Then he went to the chair where the clergyman had been sitting, and took out cigarettes.

"Smoke?"

Tiger didn't speak, and Ross lit a cigarette.

"Sit down, Tiger, and be yourself, or you'll really run into trouble."

Tiger gulped, moved round the desk, trod in the pool of ink and did not notice it. He reached his chair and dropped down. The rage had faded into bewilderment, making his eyes looked dazed; his mouth still gaped. He took a dirty handkerchief from his pocket and began to dab at his lips.

"I shouldn't try any funny business with the parson," Ross said. "He has a lot of friends you wouldn't know about. But I didn't come to talk about him or the Mission, Tiger. Who paid you to send Cary to open my safe?"

"*Cary,*" sighed Tiger, and closed his eyes. "S'welp me, I must be dreaming."

"You're awake," said Ross. "You sent Cary to my flat— who paid you?"

Tiger didn't answer, but stopped dabbing at his lips and looked more wary. The buffing sound started up again outside. Ross tapped the ash from his cigarette into an over-full tin lid which served as an ash-tray.

"Open up, Tiger, or you'll really get hurt. This is a murder rap. I'm not interested in seeing you swing, but I want to see the other man dangle. Who was it?" He leaned forward and lifted the telephone, the only modern thing in the office. "The Yard number is Whitehall 1212, isn't it? Better tell me, before I call them, Tiger."

He began to dial.

CHAPTER 14
SAMMY BRAY

Tiger watched Ross's finger in the dialling holes, and when he had reached the first 1, stretched out an unsteady hand and touched Ross's wrist. There was no venom in his eyes or his movement, he looked shaken out of his wits. Ross paused.

"Who paid you, Tiger?"

"Just put that telephone dahn, mister, we'll 'ave a little chat," said Tiger.

Ross put the receiver down.

"Thanks," said Tiger, and wiped his forehead. "You—you Ross?"

"That's right."

"And you caught Cary?"

"That's right."

"And"—Tiger drew his breath—"and he squealed."

"That's right," said Ross. "The same way as you'll squeal and for the same reason, because I put on the pressure. Like to see a Yard man come in? Like to be up before the beak in the morning for assaulting that parson? I think I could make sure you were inside for six months, and while you were away the police would have a good look round here and some of your other spots. It will pay you to talk and then take it easy."

Ross stubbed out his cigarette, but didn't look away from Tiger's eyes.

Tiger said: "Sure, sure, Mister. I don't want any more days like this."

He hesitated, as if exhausted—then leapt out of his chair and smashed a blow at Ross with a spanner he'd taken from the floor.

He missed.

Ross hit him twice on the point, hammer blows which knocked him silly. Tiger slid back into his chair, and Ross went round to the front of the desk and pulled open several drawers, running quickly through the contents, with Tiger's stertorous breathing giving unmusical accompaniment.

He found a note-book, with some names and telephone numbers, and one was Sammy Bray's. In another book were notes of payments made to different people, and there were two recent entries, reading:

"Cary—£10."

"Cary—£15."

Tiger was beginning to take notice again.

"Like some more, or are you going to talk?" asked Ross. "Why send Cary to my flat?"

"I—I never," Tiger muttered. " 'E did a job for a man I know. 'E just said 'e wanted a guy to do a job, Cary's aht of work, I wanted to 'elp 'im."

"Very touching," said Ross. "Who's the man?"

"He calls hisself——"

"I don't want to know what he calls himself, I want to know who he is." Ross leaned forward. "Tiger, I can smash you up, break your garage and your racket, and make sure you see the inside of a jail for a long time. And I might be able to make you swing. This is a murder rap, remember I told you so. Whom did Cary do that job for?"

"'E calls hisself Kelly," said Tiger, in a sighing voice, "but 'is name's Bray, Sammy Bray."

"That had better be true," Ross said.

He stood up swiftly, and before Tiger could speak again, was at the door. He touched his forehead in a mock salute, and went out. The mechanics and the youth were all staring at the door, and looked away quickly as Ross strode out. Ross walked towards the big garage doors, but didn't go far. He swung round and went back, without a sound, reached the office door and turned the handle, pulling so that he could just see inside.

Tiger sat back in his chair, a hand at his lips, staring blankly at the opposite wall; his hand was nowhere near the telephone.

The battling cleric was sitting at the wheel of the sports car, just along the road. He grinned at Ross, who drove his own car across and got out. They met outside the Mission. The clergyman was dabbing at his knuckles with a handkerchief which was snow white where it wasn't stained red. Outside, he looked not only tall and powerful, but also very young.

"Sorry about that," he said.

"Sorry! It couldn't have been better, you softened Tiger up, and I got what I wanted."

"What did you want?"

"Oh, this and that. You pack a nice punch."

"I haven't let myself go like that for a couple of years," said the other. "My name's Abbott. Tiger's been a nuisance ever since I came here, he tries to stop the youngsters from coming to my club. The row had to blow up, sooner or later, but I doubt if I used the right methods this time."

"I don't," said Ross. "If he gives you any more trouble, just say 'Ross' to him, and I think he'll be angelic."

"What's your magic?" asked Abbott.

Ross grinned.

"He thinks he may have done something which could get him hanged."

"That wouldn't surprise me," said Abbott. "Look here, cheek and all that, but you don't know Tiger or this district, do you?"

"No."

"I've only been here a few months, but that's long enough to know that Tiger can be dangerous. I can't understand why the police leave him alone. He's probably smart, and beat the rap every time, but—he's dangerous. Don't take anything for granted with him."

"I don't think he'll give us much trouble," said Ross. "If you run into any with him, give me a ring, will you?" He handed Abbott his card. "And thanks for softening him up."

"Pleasure," said Abbott. "I live two doors along, Number Fourteen."

"No manse or vicarage?"

"It was blitzed, and anyhow, I'm better placed living among them than in a palace. Anything I can do for you?"

"Not now," said Ross, "but there may be."

They shook hands, and Abbott watched him drive off.

He entered his flat more cautiously, but this time there was nothing in the way of surprises. He went to the telephone and reported to Craigie, who hadn't yet any reports about Bray, Dolly Leeming, or Barnard; they agreed that it looked as if Barnard was out, Bray was the only man they need worry about. Perry had reported that Cary had gone to his own flat; the police knew that he often did odd jobs for Tiger.

"Tiger may have tipped Bray off," Ross said, thoughtfully.

"I doubt it. If Tiger cracked like that, he's probably washed his hands of the job. That's how he works, and how he keeps clear of the police," Craigie said. "He's known to be as bad as they come but has a nice build-up of legitimate business, and usually has an alibi or a sound legal excuse. As now—he'll stick to the story that he put a job in Cary's way and didn't know what the job was. He'll probably have two or three eye-witnesses to prove it, too. Tiger is a nasty piece of work, but not really dangerous—he scares too easily, and he'd sell his own wife if it would keep him out of jail."

"I hope you're right," said Ross. "So he's married."

Craigie laughed.

"Does it matter?"

"I don't know, yet. I'll tell you what I do know, Gordon."

"Yes?"

"If Bray has to use men of Tiger's type, he's not so good as he seemed to be."

"Don't take that for granted," said Craigie. "He may have wanted to switch the attention away from himself to Tiger—he wouldn't know that Tiger would crack so easily.

He might not want to use his own men for a job like the attack on you and the flat raids. Bray isn't the man who spoke to you on the telephone, is he?"

"No, I'd recognise the voice."

"It's the man behind Bray we're after," Craigie said.

Ross nodded, as if the other could see him, said: "All right, I'll go and see Bray this evening," and rang off.

He sat back in an easy chair, and pondered. He wanted Mae back and Alice back, but that was no longer the main objective. They were being used in the effort to get hold of Conway—and also in the effort to stop him from working on the case, and presumably the reason he was wanted off duty was that he could trace Bray.

Could there be any other reason?

He couldn't think of one.

Half an hour later, Craigie telephoned with the latest information about Bray; and they made their plans.

Dolly Leeming was in a gay mood when she left her tiny flat, near Shepherd's Market, to go to Bray's. She had reason to be gay, for her fortunes had changed remarkably since Bray had become serious and started to talk of marriage.

A man walked up to her.

"Mind coming with me?" he asked, and showed a Special Branch card.

Sammy Bray looked a happy man.

There were many reasons why he should be happy, for he was known to be wealthy; as gardeners sometimes have green fingers, so Bray's were touched with gold. He had only to finger a project to make a small fortune out of it. He had genius, too, in that he managed to make the most of his money in legal ways which kept the eager grasp of the Treasury off it. He did not, as far as anyone knew, commit any crime, or even side-track the Commissioners of Inland Revenue. He succeeded because of his bland 'honesty' and the fact that he always had an answer for everything.

Another reason was the fact that he had many friends. True, most of these were fair-weather friends, but it did not greatly matter, because for Sammy Bray the barometer was always set fair, so he could rely on keeping his friends.

There was, moreover, another quality in him, which most people saw quickly; he had a genuine geniality. He had a ready if bluff wit and a kindly temperament; he was, in fact, soft-hearted. While not remarkably free with his money, he seldom failed to respond to a plea for help from a deserving friend or acquaintance. People from charwomen to porters, peers of the realm, and unlucky actors and actresses had reason to bless Sammy Bray for his generosity.

He made a rule never to lend money; loans, he was fond of saying, simply cut friendship. So, he gave. Consequently, many people in quite influential places, and who had the ear of important people, had reason to be grateful to him. They did not hesitate to perform any service they could for Sammy. He had never been known to ask for too much; rather, for too little.

Basking in the sunlight of many friends and reclining on the downy upholstery of a great deal of money, Sammy added to his happiness by falling in love.

He did this in the easy, genial way one would expect of him; he was not passionate or demanding, but as pleased with romance as a schoolgirl with her first calf-love, although nothing like so intense. In Dolly Leeming he had found a 'girl' who answered practically every one of his requirements. She wasn't bad looking, and she had a nice figure—a little cushiony, but Sammy was plump himself, and was fond of curves. She had little in the way of a mind, although she had a native wit and intelligence which enabled them to see many things in the same way, and to laugh at the same things. Dolly was not malicious, and she also had a kind heart. Those who knew them well said that it was an excellent match and, knowing Sammy, were sure that it would not be long before invitations to the wedding were sent out. It was likely to be a slap-up wedding.

Sammy had a luxurious flat in London, near Park Lane, and a 'little cottage' in Surrey, where he kept a staff of four servants and two gardeners, whether he was in residence or not. He gave many parties at the Surrey house, which was Welcome Hall to practically anyone who had any excuse to go there for a free meal, free drinks, and whirl of gaiety which at no time exceeded the limits of decency. Sammy could be *risqué* and daring, but was never obscene.

He was not known to have any strong political leanings or any serious thought of politics or world affairs. He looked after Number One, and let all the other numbers look after themselves, within the limits of his generosity.

These were all the things that were generally known about him; and these were summarised in the report which Gordon Craigie had gathered, at short notice, and which Ross received before he set out to pay his call on Sammy Bray. There was nothing at all in the report to suggest that Bray was known to be an associate of Willy Tiger.

A small point was cleared up; Cary had gone out, early that morning, with his brother-in-law, with whom he shared a flat. They often worked together.

Sammy Bray also had offices in the Strand—small but palatial. He was not a producer, just a financier; there were many who said that if Sammy Bray were on to a new thing, it was worth a fortune to be on his back while he went into it. There were countless visitors to his office and his London flat, and all of them brought little odds and ends of financial news from all parts of the globe. He was, in his way, a kind of financial Gordon Craigie. How wealthy he was was anyone's guess. In spite of everything that was known about him, he was not regarded as a modern Croesus, partly because he did not make a god of money. He was the Happy Warrior of finance.

On that afternoon, he sat alone in his palatial office, drinking tea from an exquisite Sèvres cup which stood on an exquisite silver tray, itself standing on a superb walnut desk. The walnut panelling of the walls had a soft lustre, the lighting was all concealed, and there was little to suggest the financial magnate—except the hush and the obvious wealth of the man who owned the offices.

He was smiling delightedly.

His round face was pink, rather than red, he had grey eyes which twinkled a lot, a baby mouth, and nothing much in the way of a chin. The best tailor in London cut his clothes, and the best bootmaker in London made his shoes; he had small, neat feet. His taste in shirts and ties was discreet, there was nothing showy about him.

He was in a good mood because, even as he sipped tea and afterwards munched cream cakes and *confiserie* which could be obtained in only three places in London, he was looking at a little note which Dolly had written to him; Dolly had a habit of writing little *billets doux* so that he received one when he did not expect to—and that pleased the simple part of his mind. He finished his tea, smoothed back his hair—what little he had was silky and light brown, turning grey discreetly and almost imperceptibly—and rang the bell for his second secretary, who was middle-aged and frighteningly efficient.

"Are there any more letters to sign, Miss Webb?"

"No." She picked up the tray. "Have you finished?"

"Thank you—thank you, yes. Then I think I will go home, there isn't likely to be anything else, is there?"

"I don't think so," said Miss Webb, whose hatchet face would have alarmed anyone who did not know her. "There's this."

She put a note on the desk, and whisked out.

It was a small note in a sealed envelope, and there was only Sammy's name on the envelope. His smile faded, and he looked older. He frowned as he picked it up, and then slit the envelope open with a silver paper-knife.

There was a single fold of note-paper inside, and a few lines of writing; there was no address and no signature.

"Ross saw Tiger this afternoon. I don't trust Tiger as far as I can see him."

Sammy pursed his lips, and turned them into a little pink rosebud, screwed the note up and lit a corner of it, from a lighter. He held it until the flames threatened his fingers, then dropped it into an ash-tray and watched it burn until it was just a screw of charred paper. He put this into the waste-paper basket, where it broke into a hundred tiny pieces. He was still frowning—and it was not until he left his office and was visible to the girls and men in the outer offices, that the smile returned; no one would have said that he was in any way worried.

His black Daimler and his navy-blue-uniformed chauffeur were waiting for him outside.

"Home, sir?" asked the chauffeur.

"Please."

Sammy beamed and nodded, and when he sat back in his corner, the smile faded and the frown replaced it. He lit a cigarette, and stubbed it out almost at once. He scowled at the passing people, and scowled more darkly whenever they were held up in a traffic block.

When he reached the block of flats, a huge one which was known to have the highest rentals in London, the scowl had vanished. The two porters and three neighbours whom he passed on his way to the flat all received a beaming smile. To all outward appearances Sammy was himself.

His chauffeur took the car round to the garage, where he would wait for further instructions.

Sammy reached the door of his flat, on the second floor, and was surprised; usually the door was opened as he reached it, for the porter telephoned Watson, his manservant, to say that he was on his way up. He hesitated for a few seconds, before realising that the door was not going to be opened for him so simply. He rang the bell; nothing happened. He frowned again, and took out his keys.

Then a smile broke through the frown, and this time it was a genuine one; he understood! Dolly was here, planning one of her little surprises; she would have told his man not to open the door. It would be like her to be standing just behind the door, ready to jump and shout "Bo!" when he appeared.

He pushed the door open slowly, playfully.

There was no sign of Dolly.

Still smiling, he peered round the door, preparing to startle her as she would love to startle him; but all he saw was the wall and a picture of Picasso; Sammy bought only the best pictures by all the best artists.

He closed the door, and called: "Watson!"

Watson, who should have materialised on the instant, didn't appear. Sammy's smile faded again, and he walked across to the drawing-room, looking forward to an easy chair and, before long, a drink.

He thrust open the door.

Ross looked up at him from his favourite arm-chair and another man, tall and gangling and with a lean face, sat on a couch with his legs up, smiling crookedly.

"Watson's out, having a chat with some friends," Ross said. "We're going to have a little chat with you."

CHAPTER 15
SAMMY BLEATS

Sammy Bray stood with a hand on the door, staring at the two men, mouth open and rounded, eyes also rounded, one hand raised a little in front of him as if he had expected something to be thrown at him. Slowly, he lowered both hands and moved farther into the room, and a tremulous smile spoilt the O of his lips.

"My dear Ross—good evening, good evening." He glanced at Williamson. "I don't think I know your friend."

"Tim," said Ross, "meet Mr. Samuel Bray—Mr. Timothy Williamson."

"*Very* glad to see you," said Bray. "A most unexpected pleasure!" He walked across to the window and stood with his back to it, considerably less than medium height, so well dressed that he looked just well built. "How *are* you, Ross?"

"Fine."

"Good!"

"How are you, Sammy?"

"Me? I've never been better," said Bray. "It's a lovely day, I'm a very happy man—I can't imagine wanting anything different. What can I do for you?"

"Where's Mae Harrison?" asked Ross.

"*Mae?*"

"That's right."

"My dear Ross, *I* don't know," said Bray. "She hasn't been to see me for some time, I only wish she had. What a lucky man you are, Ross, to be engaged to a woman like Mae!"

"Yes, aren't I? Where is she?"

"I really don't know what the joke is," said Bray, a little warily. "I suppose you'll tell me what it's all about before long, but I assure you, I have no idea where Mae is. Probably buying a new dress! Will you have a drink?"

"No, thanks. Where is she?"

"Really, Ross..."

"Don't get all indignant," said Ross. "Let me tell you a story. After Mae had been kidnapped this morning her flat was burgled—someone had taken her key. The same someone burgled my flat, afterwards, but he didn't have the same luck. I caught him. He put me on to a Mister William Tiger. Tiger told me that he'd had his instructions from you. Now whoever kidnapped Mae took her keys, and those keys were used by the burglar, who was employed by you. Where is she, Sammy?"

Bray said: *"Really!"* in a piping little voice, and ran a hand over his forehead; he was sweating, and began to look frightened. "This is absurd. Tiger? I've never heard of a man named Tiger."

"Liar."

"My dear Ross, I must insist..."

"We're doing the insisting," said Ross. "My friend and I want Mae."

"I have no idea..."

"Where Dolly Leeming is," said Ross.

Bray started violently, and his right hand went to his pocket; the others watched him closely, but he only took out a gold cigarette-case. He put a cigarette to his lips and rolled it from one side of his mouth to the other, but didn't light it. His eyes were suddenly smaller, and he didn't look so fat; he looked very nearly dangerous.

"What do you mean?"

"That you don't know where Dolly is, and I don't know where Mae is, and that fair exchange is no robbery."

Bray said softly: "Are you telling me that you've kidnapped my *Dolly?*"

"Yes," said Ross.

"The police…"

"Won't help. This is only hearsay, not evidence, and even if you had all the evidence you want, you couldn't get the police to help you on this job. Where's Mae?"

Bray went to a chair and dropped into it. Williamson stood up and, watched by the little plump man with dazed eyes, struck his lighter and held it out. Bray gulped, and said:

"Thank you, thank you. Ross, I don't understand…."

"I couldn't make it any clearer," said Ross. "When I have Mae back, I'll really talk business. For instance, who you're working for and why you've dabbled in this kind of dirt. You're supposed to have clean fingers, although we've often doubted whether that's true. Now, about Mae?"

Bray said slowly: "Where *is* Dolly?"

"Comfortable, but scared."

"You've no right…"

Ross said: "Bray, three men were killed at Shepperton last night."

"What has that got to do with me?"

"It could get you hanged."

"Oh, nonsense!"

"It isn't nonsense. You're playing in a deadly business, and you'll find out more about it as time goes on, but just now, I want to know where Mae Harrison is. When I have her safe and sound, you can have your Dolly, and we'll talk business. But Mae's the first thing."

Bray didn't answer.

He drew at his cigarette and studied the carpet between his feet; it was fawn-coloured, without any pattern. The silence in the big room was so profound that the two men could hear his breathing. Ross looked at the thin patch on top of Bray's head, and wondered what was passing through his mind. He did not know how much Bray knew, did not know whether he was dangerous or whether he was just a tool of the people who wanted Conway.

Bray looked up.

"Blackmail is an ugly thing," he said, in a bleating voice. "It's a terrible thing. I am being—blackmailed."

"You shouldn't keep skeletons in your cupboard."

"How can a man undo his past?" asked Bray, and his lips and voice trembled. He drew his hand across his forehead and drooped in his chair, as if the life had been drained out of him. He looked like nothing more than a disappointed and frightened child; the change was fascinating. "Ross, I hoped I should never have to confess to any man that—that I made my start in life—dishonestly."

Williamson and Ross exchanged glances.

"Poor chap," said Williamson.

"It may be funny to you," said Bray, "but I assure you that it is not funny so far as I am concerned. It is—a tragedy. I have been haunted by my past throughout the years."

"You've hidden it fairly well," said Ross.

"Yes, yes, I have put on a bold face. I am temperamentally a happy and easily contented man, and nature will out. I do not propose at this stage to tell you what I did or how I broke the law, but—this is the simple truth—for some months I have been blackmailed."

"By whom?"

"I do not know," said Bray, and his voice dropped almost to a whisper. "I do not know his name, but—he has given me several ultimatums. It has been a shrewd and cruel business, because the man has not asked for money, which I could easily pay, but for—my services."

"Such as?"

"The demands have varied," Bray said in a tremulous voice. "I have been asked to give information on the financial status of certain men."

"What men?"

Bray closed his eyes.

"Politicians—statesmen—permanent officials at various ministries. Men in high positions."

"And you've given the information?"

"For what I imagined to be my own peace of mind, yes," Bray said. He opened his eyes, and it looked as if there were tears in them. "I know a great deal about finance, I know the rich and the poor and those who are putting up a show which they really cannot afford. My business is money, and I have to know the financial status of everyone with whom I do business, and it was not difficult for me to find out what this man wanted to know."

"You're sure it's a man?" asked Ross.

"Yes, yes. He has spoken to me on the telephone, but I cannot be sure that I have been dealing with the principal. He is a man I do not know, as I have told you. Yesterday, his demands took on a new aspect, in its way—sinister. Yes, sinister," breathed Bray, and again his lips quivered. "He asked me to report on—you."

"Ah," said Ross.

"And your beloved."

Williamson smothered a laugh and turned it into a snort, and Bray opened his eyes and looked at him sadly.

"Little is sacred to you, Mr. Williamson, I can see that. The young have so little regard for the higher things in life, it is one of the sad facts about the new generation, and I think it is part of the explanation of the unhappy state of the world. Be that as it may, Ross, I was asked to report on you and on your fiancée. I was asked to find out whether there were any stresses and strains, whether you seemed perfectly happy or not, and—and a strange thing was added."

"What?"

Bray looked fully into Ross's eyes, and chose his words with great care.

"Believe me or not, I was told that I must find a way of coming between you. That I must, somehow, cause emotional trouble for you. Do not ask me why I was selected for that melancholy task. I received those instructions last evening, and when I went to the Dive and saw you, believe me I was heavy hearted—a very sad man. And then you quarrelled!" Bray raised his hands. "Without any prompting from me, you quarrelled—and I was greatly relieved. There was no *need* for me to do what the man wanted, it had already been done for him. I knew that I only had to report, and that I would be free of at least one weight upon my conscience."

"Ah," said Ross, heavily. "And then?"

"And then he telephoned me again, late last night. I had to obtain for him the services of a man who could pick locks and open safes. He told me to get in touch with a man in the East End—this Tiger. Tiger supplied such a criminal. I told this man, through Tiger, to raid your flat, and go to Miss Harrison's flat this morning. These were my instructions."

Bray stopped.

"And that's all?" asked Ross.

Bray did not answer immediately, but pressed his hands against his forehead and stared at Ross; and his eyes looked glazed and glassy, he had lost colour. Williamson moved slowly across the room, but Bray took no notice of him, appeared to be completely obsessed with what he was saying.

"That is not quite all, Ross. The man telephoned me again, this morning. He said that I was not to be surprised if I heard that Mae Harrison had disappeared, and that I was not to say a word to you, to the police, or anyone. For my own safety, I promised that I would not. Then later, I had a warning that you had seen Tiger, Ross. I knew then that if you came to me, I should not have the strength of mind to keep quiet. Finding you here was a great shock—a very great shock. I knew I should have to talk, and I have told you everything I can. Everything."

CHAPTER 16
DEAD END

The story answered almost any question they might want to ask about Bray and told them nothing they wanted to know about Mae. The plump little man sat in that attitude of absolute dejection, his eyes glassy with the strain; that might be good acting. He made no appeal, seemed to realise that it would be a waste of time.

Ross said: "When Mae's back, you can have Dolly."

"Ross!"

The word was agonised.

"I'm not in this business for my health," said Ross.

"What—business—are—you—in?"

"Never mind."

Bray stood up slowly, and went to a cabinet, opened it, and fumbled with bottles. He took one out, but didn't unstopper it, just turned to face Ross.

"I know a little about you, of course. Your mysterious errands, some of the people you know, where you go. I've always guessed that you were in the Secret Service."

"Have you? Why?"

"I have to know these things," said Bray vaguely.

"I don't see why."

Bray smoothed the bottle with his left hand.

"I need to know everything I can. Ross, you wouldn't hurt Dolly. Whatever you are, whatever you're doing, you wouldn't harm my darling Dolly."

"Wouldn't I?"

Bray closed his eyes, and muttered: "You're not human!"

"I want Mae, and I want the man who kidnapped her, for more things than that job. And until I have them, you can't rest in peace about your darling Dolly. Not that I think you care a rap for her. You're a smooth liar, but still a liar."

"I have told the simple truth." A hint of dignity crept into Bray's manner now. He took out the stopper and went back for glasses, poured out three nips and picked up the soda siphon. He had perfect control over his movements, although he hardly seemed aware of what he was doing. "If you hurt that girl——"

"It's a hard life," said Ross. "Three people have been murdered."

"I did not know that."

"It's true. And one more life won't make much difference. You've guessed what I am, and you may have guessed wrong. You know I mean what I say—no Mae, no Dolly."

"I can do *nothing* to help you."

"You can."

"Tell me—how."

"This mystery man will get in touch with you again. Arrange to meet him."

"I've often tried, but he won't come into the open."

"Try again," said Ross. "Think of Dolly."

Bray said: "I will try, but I don't think it will do any good."

"Then nothing will," said Ross.

"How will you know when we meet?" asked Bray, after a pause.

"I'll know," Ross said.

Bray nodded, sadly, and lifted a glass, looked at it, and drank. Only then did he realise that he hadn't given the others their drinks. He looked pathetically apologetic as he brought them across.

"Thanks," said Ross, "but I'll start drinking your health when I know where Mae is."

He went out; and Williamson followed swiftly. Neither of them glanced at the plump little man who stood with bowed head and the glass in his hand.

Ross tried the old trick, slamming the door without properly closing it. Williamson went towards the front door, making plenty of noise, while Ross stepped back to this one, and opened it an inch. Bray wasn't moving; but he might suspect the trick. Ross backed away again, closing the door very gently, gave the man sixty seconds, and then tried again. Bray was standing in exactly the same position, and had a crushed, defeated look.

Ross joined Williamson, outside.

"Shall I keep tabs on him?"

"Will you, Tim? I'll arrange with Craigie to send someone else, and have you relieved a bit later."

"Right. Believe him?"

"I can't be sure."

"He loves his Dolly," said Williamson. "Whether he thinks you'll harm her is a different matter. He'll probably call your bluff."

"We'll see," said Ross.

Bray's man, Watson, was downstairs; he had been questioned, seemed to know nothing. Ross let him return to his master.

When Ross went into his flat, the telephone bell was ringing. He answered it right away, and was prepared for the smooth voice of the man who had given no name. There was a difference; it was a harsher voice in some ways, and he did not think the man was pleased.

"Ross?"

"Speaking."

"I've warned you."

"The twelve hours isn't up yet."

"It won't be long."

"That's right," said Ross.

"You won't get anything out of Bray, because he doesn't know anything."

"What else did he say?"

"For a man who talks so much normally, he was very reticent," said Ross. "But he'll talk. There's one thing you've forgotten, stranger."

"I am not forgetful by nature."

Ross laughed, explosively.

"I shouldn't like to say what you are by nature, but you're a fool in most ways. If I throw my hand in, others will take up the job."

"I'll deal with the others."

"You certainly think you're good," said Ross. "Listen— I'll talk business when Mae's back."

"You'll talk business before that," the man said, and rang off.

His calls were local calls; so he was in London, somewhere within the dialling area. That meant they had only to search among the million-odd telephone subscribers to find him—unless he borrowed someone else's telephone and used a different one each time. He was rattled; that had revealed itself in his voice. But he knew that Ross had seen Bray, and that meant he was keeping a close watch on the little man. Ross had seen no one at or near the mansion block who might have reported; but a porter would do, a next-door neighbour—there were dozens of possibilities.

Ross sent for dinner from a nearby restaurant, after making arrangements with Craigie for Bray to be watched. Everything now depended on whether Bray managed to see the mystery man. Would the unknown fall for it?

Ross doubted it.

He did not enjoy his dinner.

He'd just finished when the telephone bell rang again, and it was Brown, who had gone to join Williamson in the watch on Bray.

"Peter?"

"Bray had a drink at the Dive, left twenty minutes ago, met a man at the corner of Regent Street and Great Marlborough Street, and they went off together in a taxi. Tim's following in a radio-equipped car. Be ready for a call."

"I'm ready," said Ross, softly.

"So'm I," said Brown, and rang off.

Williamson called over the radio, which was operated at Scotland Yard. Bray had left the other man after they had ridden for fifteen minutes. Bray was still in the taxi, the other man was walking along the Strand. Brown was walking after him, Williamson following slowly in the car.

Ross caught up with Williamson's car at the corner of Chancery Lane.

"Along here," Williamson said as Ross drew up.

Ross pulled the car in, left it parked at the kerbside, and Williamson to deal with any police protest, and walked swiftly along Chancery Lane. Its narrow length was almost deserted. He saw a man pass beneath a lighted window, and again beneath a street lamp; then the man was swallowed up in the darkness. A car came along, its headlights blazing, and there was no sign of the man. Ross hurried, and as he passed the doorway of a building near Holborn, he heard Brown whisper:

"Here."

Brown was inside the doorway of the building.

"He came in here." Brown's voice was pitched very low, as Ross turned into the doorway. "He didn't use a key for this door, and I heard him walk up the stairs."

"Good. Know the place?"

"Not to say know it. There are several small firms here—nothing of any consequence." Brown glanced up at a board with the names and addresses of the firms in the building. "I've read them."

"Back way?" asked Ross.

"I don't know."

"Will you go and see?"

Brown nodded, and disappeared with his astonishing silence of movement. Ross went to the front door and tried the handle; the door was locked. He took out his skeleton key, but hesitated, then touched the keyhole lightly with the metal, half-expecting to get an electric shock; it wouldn't be as simple as this.

There was no shock.

If he picked the lock, there might be an alarm.

He worked on the lock, and found himself tense and cold. There was no way of being sure that this was the man who telephoned; no way of being sure that if he were, then Mae was here. He felt the key get a hold and turned gently.

The door opened.

Brown appeared as if out of thin air.

"Only back way is the window, and Tim's out there."

"Good."

Ross thrust the door open a foot, and squeezed through. There was no light beyond. He didn't use a torch, but stood for long enough to get his eyes accustomed to the gloom. Then he moved forward, with Brown close on his heels. He could pick out the staircase and the pale-coloured walls, reached the bottom step and started up. They were wooden steps without any covering; no one could go up without making some noise.

Even Brown made a few creaks, but so few that they couldn't be heard unless someone was close at hand listening for them. As they reached the first landing, a faint glow of light showed through the window. Ross reached it and peered out; there was no sign of Williamson.

Was this a waste of time?

Brown was already half-way up the stairs. They saw no glimmer of light until they reached the next landing; then it came from the floor above—from the top of a closed door. Ross put his hand to his pocket and his gun. Brown was still in the lead, moving with uncanny silence.

He reached the next landing.

He stepped forward—and a bell rang, sharp and shrill, beyond the door.

There was a moment of tense silence, and then a thud—and the light went out. Ross launched himself at the door, it creaked and sagged but didn't open. Brown joined him, they strained at it together—and as it creaked there was another sound; a scream.

The door crashed open.

Brown staggered into the darkness beyond, and the scream was repeated; a woman was in there. Ross stood swiftly to one side and Brown called:

"I'm okay."

The woman screamed again, as if in agony—and then her voice gurgled away into silence—an uncanny and frightening silence.

No one spoke.

Brown shifted his position slightly.

A man said in the familiar telephone voice:

"Let me go, or I'll kill her."

There was no noisy menace, just the simple statement—
of a man who meant exactly what he said. Ross didn't answer,
and tried to pierce the gloom. He could make out the shape
of another door, but there was no glimmer of light.

"Understand, Ross?" the man said.

Ross didn't answer.

"You needn't think you'll break my nerve," said the man.
"Let me go, or I'll kill her. Come in—with your hands in sight."

Ross kept silent.

The man said: "Listen," and after a pause there was
another scream, so close to them, so agonised, that it sent
a palsy of cold fear up Ross's spine. It was choked off into a
gurgle, and there was a sound, as of a body falling.

Then a light stabbed out from a torch. It shone through
the other door, which had been opened, Ross could see only
the bright orb and the beam. He couldn't even see Brown,
who had moved to one side.

"Do what I tell you, Ross," the man said.

Ross took his hand from his pocket and his gun and
stepped forward. The light was shining on to his chest, and the
glow spread to his face. Apart from that, there was blackness.
He took another step—and then darted to one side. A shot
roared out, flame stabbed. Ross hit the wall, lost his balance,
and the man in the dark room rushed forward, firing again.

Ross heard a gasp from Brown—and Brown fell against
him, stopping him from getting at his gun. The gunman
jumped to the head of the stairs, fired twice again, and then
raced down.

Brown gave a curious rattling sound in his throat.

Ross turned, in pursuit.

Chapter 17
Rescue

Ross fired as he reached the top of the stairs, and the flash showed the running man, half-way down the next flight. He was turning, with his gun pointed upwards. Ross lost precious seconds flattening himself against the wall. A bullet thudded close to his head. The man ran on. Ross took a chance and swung himself over the banisters, landed on the edge of a step, and fell. He didn't hurt himself, and was up in a flash. The running man fired again, but aimed too high. Ross fired at the flash.

Then he trod on the edge of a step, and fell heavily.

He heard the other's thudding footsteps, but no other sound. Even that faded. He picked himself up, and hurried down. A cool breeze came in at the open door, and he saw the dim lights of Chancery Lane. Two or three people were hurrying towards Holborn, and stood back when they saw him.

The man had disappeared.

"What's up?" a man asked.

"What's *that?*" cried a girl.

A car turned into the street, and its bright lights shone on spots which glistened bright red—blood. There were several of them on the white step, close to Ross; so he'd winged his man.

135

"Say, what *is* all this?" a man asked, nervously.

"Police," said Ross, and turned and ran towards Holborn, breathing more easily. A policeman loomed up as he reached the corner.

Ross showed his card.

"Special Branch. Did you see a man running from here just now?"

"I did, sir, he got into a taxi, and went that way."

The constable pointed.

"Call the Information Room, tell them about it—the man's wounded. He's wanted for murder."

Ross didn't give the man time to react, ignored the gasps of the little crowd that had gathered, bored his way through it, and went back to the building. As he reached the entrance, Williamson appeared from the other direction.

"Luck?"

"Some," said Ross. "Brown's hurt."

Williamson made no comment, and they went upstairs, switching on the lights as they went. From the first floor landing downwards there were spots of blood; the man seemed to have been wounded badly. The lights shone on the unpainted walls and the white-painted doors, all of which were closed. There was no sound upstairs.

Brown lay in a huddled heap, with a bullet hole in his forehead.

Ross motioned to him, and Williamson stopped; Ross didn't see the tall man's face. He went into the rooms from which the man had run, and switched on the light. The first room was an office with two desks in it, several filing-cabinets, and a large cupboard. He opened the cupboard doors; there were shelves, papers, and books inside, no one was there. He set his teeth as he stepped into the next door, and the scream from the girl seemed to echo about him, even now. He groped for and pressed down the light.

It was Mae.

She was tied to an upright chair, lolling forward, fully dressed although her blouse was torn at the shoulder and one sleeve had been ripped out, showing her long, bare arm. She didn't move.

Ross tried to relax as he went towards her, but he couldn't. He felt a surge of hatred and of anger with himself—that he had let the man go. He raised Mae's head, gently. Her eyes were closed, and her lips were parted. She was horridly pale, had on practically no lipstick—he'd never seen her look anything like this. He cut the cords at her wrists and legs; this was the third time he'd done that, the man was an expert in tying up his victims.

Mae slumped forward.

Ross lifted her bodily and carried her across the room to a large arm-chair; this was a private office, furnished with some comfort. He pulled up another chair and rested her legs on it, and pushed a pillow behind her head so that she could lie comfortably. He touched her wrist, hesitated, and felt for the pulse; then smiled grimly at himself, for there was no need for that, she was breathing. He felt her head, gingerly; there was no lump, nothing to suggest that she had a head wound. He took out his flask and forced a trickle of brandy between her lips. She gulped at once, and swallowed most of the brandy; her eyes flickered.

Ross stood back, lighting a cigarette.

Williamson was talking on the telephone in the other room, presumably to Craigie.

Ross went out, and looked at Brown, although he knew that Brown was dead. Williamson put down the receiver and stretched out his hand for a cigarette; Ross gave him one, without speaking.

"How's the girl? Was it Mae?"

"Yes. She'll do."

"I heard the shout."

"I don't know what he did to her," said Ross, "but I know what I'll do to him."

"That trail of blood should help."

"Yes. Gordon sending a doctor?"

Williamson nodded.

"And Loftus is coming himself, I think."

Ross shrugged and went back into the inner room. Mae was still leaning back, but her lips were closed, there was a tinge of colour in her cheeks, her eyes flickered. Ross took her hand and squeezed gently, and her eyes opened wider. They were surprisingly clear and lovely, but dazed. She didn't seem to recognise him at first, but when she did, she moved her right hand towards him.

He took it, and pressed.

"You'll be all right, my darling."

"Peter!"

"Just take it easy."

"That man——"

"He's gone," said Ross.

"Did you—catch him?"

"We will, soon."

She closed her eyes.

"So you let him go," she said, and there was bitterness in her husky voice. "You let him——"

"Take it easy, darling." He poured out a little more brandy, and she took it eagerly. She couldn't have been tied up for long, there were no marks at her wrists, and she seemed to be in no pain from the blood re-circulating. She gasped as she finished the brandy, and held out her hand. He lit a cigarette for her, and put it between her lips. "We'll soon have you home."

"Yes. Peter, I—I'm sorry."

"Forget it."

"I didn't mean——"

"I said, forget it."

She smiled slightly, and closed her eyes again. He did not attempt to make her talk for a few minutes, but when he judged that she had recovered sufficiently and that the brandy was doing its work, he pulled up a chair and sat astride it, leaning forward on to the back.

"Better?"

"Much."

"How long have you been here, Mae?"

"Only—a few hours."

"Did he bring you?"

"Yes. Those two men yesterday took me to a house in the East End. I was locked in a room, a tiny room without windows, I could hardly breathe. They didn't—hurt me. Then he came this evening, and took me away. At the point of a gun. Peter, it's hard to believe that it happened to me."

"It won't, again."

She shuddered.

"He sat here most of the time, with the gun in his hand."

"Was anyone else with him?"

"No."

Ross asked: "You sure?"

"Of course I'm sure!"

Williamson reached the room, nodded to Mae and Ross, and went out; soon they heard him talking to one of the men who was coming up the stairs. Someone gave an order crisply, to force each office door. Ross turned back to Mae, and sat down again.

"What did he do?"

"When the burglar alarm sounded, he went out," said Mae. "He kept me covered with the gun, and I—Peter, I *hate* myself! I was so frightened. I could have cried out, but I let him do what he wanted."

"You shouldn't hate yourself," said Ross gently. He knew that someone else had come in—and from the deliberate and heavy footsteps, judged that it was Bill Loftus. He didn't look round, and Mae only glanced up. He could imagine the big man standing in the doorway, listening, deciding not to interrupt. "What happened then?"

"He knew you were there, came back, and—twisted my wrist. It was—agony. He hardly seemed to touch me, but it was as if my arm was on fire. I couldn't help screaming—Peter, I couldn't help it!"

"Now take it easy," said Ross. "I know that grip."

"And so do I," said Loftus.

He moved forward, looking burly and ungainly, smiled at Mae—and transformed himself. Smiling, he didn't look the same man, became human and likeable, like a big boy. He sat on the corner of a small desk, which tipped up a little, and he sat farther back on to it.

"Nice to see you again," he said mildly. "Thank Peter, it was his idea."

"I know," she said. "I knew that if anyone rescued me, it would be—Peter." She looked tired now, her head seemed heavy. "You're all right, aren't you?"

"I'm fine," said Ross. "Now, what did the gent look like?"

She hesitated.

"A rough description will do," said Loftus.

"Rough! I could pick him out of a thousand men," said Mae. "He's rather tall and thin—nearly as tall as that man who was here just now."

"Tim," said Ross.

"I don't know what you call him. He's very dark, going grey at the sides. His face——" She hesitated, and closed her eyes again.

The others didn't speak.

She said: "He has a long face and a high forehead, and his hair recedes at the front. He has big eyes, dark brown—they seemed uncanny. Smoky eyes." Her voice rose, she seemed almost hysterical. "I can't help it, but they seemed to smoke as if they were on fire."

"Take it easy," Loftus said.

"I—I'm sorry. He has a short nose and wide nostrils, distended at the sides. You know what I mean—nipped just above the nostrils and very wide. And thin lips, a pointed chin—a very long chin." She raised one hand. "It doesn't sound anything, but the effect——"

"We've got the effect," said Loftus. "It's fine—we'll soon have him. How are you feeling?"

"I'm all right," said Mae. She tried to get up, but collapsed. "I'll be all right in a moment."

"Will you take her home, Peter?" asked Loftus. "We'll look after things here."

"Yes. Mae, was there anyone else at this place in the East End—where you were first held?"

"Only—an old woman."

"Not another girl? A young girl, early twenties?"

Mae looked puzzled.

"No—no, I didn't see anyone like that. Why?"

"Forget it," said Loftus. "Did you know what part of the East End this was in?"

She shook her head.

"I hardly noticed anything. They stopped me at the side of the road, bundled me into a car, and made me sit back— it was a big car, I couldn't see much, because the blinds were down. I know it was the East End, I saw a drab little street of small houses. There was a garage, I remember, but I only caught a glimpse of it."

Ross said tensely: "Just a garage? Did you see another big building?"

"I—I don't think so. I was so frightened, Peter. I couldn't help it, I was anxious to do just what they told me, I was afraid of them. I used to think I could stand anything, I've never been frightened like that before. The garage was a large tin shed. They took me into a house nearby."

"Any ideas?" Loftus asked.

"I'm full of ideas," said Ross. He took Mae's hand and pressed it tightly, then brushed her forehead with his lips. "I've another little job, darling. One of the others will take you home and look after you until I get back. I won't be long."

He jumped up and turned round.

"Peter!" cried Mae. "Don't go, don't take any more risks. Don't go!"

Her voice was ringing in his ears as he hurried down the stairs.

Chapter 18
Millicent Street

L oftus could move fast when he was in a hurry, and caught up with Ross at the first landing. Williamson, who had been outside the door, was already half-way down the next flight of stairs. Loftus put a hand on Ross's shoulder.

"Millicent Street?" he asked.

"It's a chance," said Ross.

"Yes. But don't rush it, I'll talk to the Divisional Police, they'll be glad to co-operate. You've time to take Mae home before we raid that garage and the houses near it."

"Fix it with someone else, will you?" asked Ross.

"All right, old chap. But give yourself half an hour before you go to Millicent Street. I'll have it surrounded within ten minutes, and I can find out if Willy Tiger owns any of the nearby houses. I'll have the information for you when you get there—ask for the Superintendent in charge. I'll have Wally Lane and Perry there, too."

"Thanks," said Ross.

He went out, with Williamson, and they walked along Chancery Lane to his car. Neither of them spoke. It was cold, and they moved briskly, Ross breathing deeply, glad to be out in the open air. He had confused pictures, of Mae as he'd first found her, of her eyes flickering, of the thought that she was dead and the realization that she was most certainly alive. He could imagine her screaming, and guess the pressure that the man had exerted—knew exactly how it could be done; he'd used the grip himself. But in finding Mae, his job wasn't over; he'd simply crossed one bridge. As he got into his car, he asked himself whether he had really rushed away because he didn't want to be distracted from his main task, or whether it was because he was desperately anxious to find a girl with a pair of remarkable blue eyes. The personal element kept intruding, and there was nothing he could do about it. He wasn't loyal to the Department, wasn't wholly loyal to Mae; he was all mixed up, and perhaps because of that, he had let the man go.

"Shall I drive?" asked Williamson.

"Will you?"

"Where?"

"We've half an hour to spare."

"I know just the pub," said Williamson, and let in the clutch. "Did Mae see the chap?"

"Yes."

Ross repeated her description, and it could not have been more vivid on his mind. Williamson slid the car through the almost deserted Fleet Street, turned into a narrow side street, and pulled up in a parking-place. Almost opposite was a public-house, with lights blazing cheerfully and an illuminated neon sign reading: *Nag's Head.* They went into the private bar, which was crowded—there were two women and about thirty men, none of whom appeared to notice the new-comers.

"I sometimes wonder whether they write with ink or whisky," said Williamson, *sotto voce.* "And what wouldn't they give to know what we've just done and are going to do?"

He forged a way to the bar, where two or three others were waiting, and several of the newspapermen glanced at them incuriously. Then with the drinks, he went across the room, where there were two vacant chairs.

They lit cigarettes.

"Just relax," said Williamson. "You're too intense on this job, Peter."

"Blame my temperament," said Ross.

"I know what to blame, but she's all right."

"Oh, yes. Alice Conway isn't, and we still want a certain fine gentleman."

"He's on the run," said Williamson confidently. "He started off with big ideas, but I don't think he has 'em now." He kept his voice low, so that he couldn't be heard by anyone near. No one was taking the slightest interest in them. "The East End police know how to close up a district like Millicent Street, and if he did go there——"

"Not likely," said Ross. "He knows I've been there and the place is suspect. It's worth trying, no more. In any case——"

He hesitated.

"Yes?"

Ross said: "I'm probably crazy, but I wouldn't have used the police for this job. We all know the East End grapevine. If there's a police concentration, they'll know all about it. A dozen runners will sneak up to Tiger and warn him—and before the police have taken up their position, he'll have got rid of anything or anyone who might make trouble for him. I think Loftus has made a mistake."

"He doesn't make many."

Ross shrugged.

He felt calmer as they left the pub, twenty minutes later. From force of habit, they stood by the car for several minutes, to make sure that no one followed them. Newspapermen had a nose for news. No one came out, but several people went in. Ross drove now, and stopped in Fleet Street, to make quite sure they weren't followed. Then he drove across Ludgate Circus, through the desolation around St. Paul's, and along the empty City streets, with the tall, grey buildings towering up on either side. Street cleaners were at work, a water-cart was droning along, splashing water into the kerb. There was no other sign of activity, no lights in any of the offices. As they turned into Aldgate, passing the old pump, London sprang to life. Neon signs flickered and glowed in a dozen colours, the Underground Station was a hubbub of activity, traffic suddenly became thick. The barrow-boys were still busy, the lighted cafés seemed crowded with people.

Ross turned towards Millicent Street, and a uniformed policeman stood in the middle of the road, hand up to stop them.

"Sorry, sir, you'll have to make a detour."

"We're on business," Ross said amiably. "Is the Superintendent in charge handy?"

He showed his Special Branch card.

"That's all right, sir, thank you. You'll find him at the other end of the street; you'd better go back, and take the next turning on the left. He doesn't want any traffic along Millicent Street just now. It's not far out of your way, sir— and it's Chief Inspector Clark."

"Thanks," said Ross.

Clark was a thick-set man with a barrel-like torso, a hoarse, whispering voice and heavy features. He showed no enthusiasm for Ross or Williamson. He wore his trilby hat at the back of his head, and kept one hand in his pocket most of the time.

"Your friends are just along there, Mr. Ross."

"Thanks. What's your plan?"

"Not *mine*," said Clark, and sounded almost bitter. "Mr. Loftus is in charge to-night."

Ross said: "Fine!" and didn't miss Clark's scowl.

He left the car and with Williamson hurried along the street. Loftus, little Perry, and Wally Lane were outside one of the small houses. The garage showed up vaguely, the Mission House was much better lighted. There were no other men in sight, although many might be hiding in doorways, perhaps even in the garage or the Mission House itself.

Loftus loomed up.

"Hallo, folks, just the right timing."

"Anything new?"

"Tiger owns the three houses next to the garage. There's a flat over the garage which his men use as a doss-house, and he lives in the third house along. He's in, all right."

"How do you want to handle him?"

"What would you do?"

Ross grinned.

"I'd just go and knock at his door and tell him I want another chat. If he hasn't already been told that there's a police crowd in the street, he might be amenable. I think I could get anything out of him that he's still keeping to himself."

"Want any company?"

"What am I here for?" asked Williamson.

Perry and Lane didn't speak or move.

"I'd say that's as good a way as any," said Loftus. "Did you reload your gun, Peter?"

"I've still three shots——"

"Better be safe," said Loftus, and handed him a clip of ammunition.

There was a light on in Tiger's house in Millicent Street; it glowed through the frosted glass of the fanlight. The small door was of solid wood. The house was exactly the same as all the others in the street, and there was no sound from it or from anywhere nearby. The police were watching at the back, there was no chance for Tiger or anyone else to get away.

Ross banged on the iron knocker, but there was no response. He knocked again, more heavily, and looked round for a bell; there wasn't one. Next time, he thundered on the knocker, but as the echoes died away, silence fell. The light still glowed.

"Tiger isn't deaf, is he?" asked Williamson mildly.

"Not yet," said Ross.

He moved towards the window and examined it; the old sash-cord type had a catch which was fastened, but might be easy to press back. He used his knife, and the blade was long enough to touch the catch; there was no need for silence, and it went back against the glass with a bang. After that, silence settled again.

He did not need to speak of the possibility of acute danger; that Tiger and perhaps others knew they were in a corner, and would try to shoot their way out. He saw Williamson put his hand to his pocket, for his gun. He pushed the window up and it squealed noisily, and he could just see the crowded furniture in the room. There was a table with an art pot and some flowers right in the window, and he had to move this aside before he climbed in.

There was no sound; the door of the room was closed.

Williamson followed him.

Ross recalled the interview with Tiger and everything that Craigie had reported about him; and there was the possibility that Craigie was wrong. As Loftus may have been wrong in using the police. The odds were that Tiger had managed to get away before the police had come.

He groped his way across the room, reached the door, and opened it cautiously.

Light shone in the passage from another room; there was no light on in the passage itself. He sidled out. The passage was only a yard wide, he could stretch out his arm and touch the far wall. There was complete silence, inside and out—the little house was empty all right.

A staircase led up from the stairs.

Ross kept close to the wall as he went towards the room where the light was on. This was at the end of the passage alongside the stairs, and probably came from the kitchen. Williamson followed, but went the other way, to open the front door. Loftus and the other Z men came in, filling the passage. Ross led the way to the kitchen. The door was only open a foot, and he could just see a dresser and a row of shelves, the corner of a table with a bottle of beer, a loaf of bread, some butter, and other oddments on it—as if Tiger had been settling down to a meal before he'd had the warning.

Ross pushed the door wider open, and saw a foot.

It was a small foot, in a canvas slipper, and its owner was lying down. The other leg was drawn up; Ross saw that as he peered cautiously round the door, not yet certain that there was nothing to fear. Then he saw the huge torso and the shirt open at the neck.

Tiger lay on his back.

Tiger's throat was cut.

Loftus looked down dispassionately, and said as if to himself:

"Well, he won't do any more harm."

He moved across the kitchen, which was as crowded as the front room. Beyond was a tiny scullery, where Ross was examining the door. The back door was locked, so no one had escaped that way. He opened it and called out to the policemen in the tiny garden, then rejoined Loftus in the kitchen. Perry was bending over Tiger's dead body, and Loftus looking through the pockets of a coat which was hanging on the back of a chair.

"Nice people," Williamson said.

"Suicide?" Perry muttered the word.

"Be yourself," said Ross. "There's no knife handy. Someone came in, and Tiger wasn't alarmed—and then he was slashed. By a friend—now we have to find all of Tiger's friends, Bill."

"Just the killer will do," said Loftus. He touched Tiger's hand. "Warm—he hasn't been dead long, but he might have been dead before you found Mae."

"Or Mae's boy friend might have come straight here," said Ross.

"Can you tell me why?"

"Not yet. Unless he was afraid we'd have another go at Tiger, who could talk. Nothing in the pockets, was there?"

"Nothing any good," said Loftus. "But it'll take us several hours to have a good look round here and at the garage. Going upstairs?"

Loftus was leaving everything to him, making it clear that it was his own show. Ross gave a twisted smile, went back and started up the stairs. He didn't expect to find anyone else here, and then remembered asking Craigie if Tiger were married. If he were, where was his wife? There was a tiny landing, and three doors led from it. Two of them stood open, and the other was closed.

He opened the closed door.

Tiger had been married; at all events, the woman on the bed, killed in exactly the same way as the man, had a wedding ring on a plump finger.

Ross glanced round, called down to tell the others, and then went into the next room. It was a small bedroom, with a single bed, and an old marble-topped washstand. It looked clean and tidy, but didn't offer him any information. He went to the third room.

Cords dangled from the posts at the foot and head of the double bed—and he didn't need telling that someone had been tied to this bed. The cords had been cut.

He stood looking round, eyes narrowed but missing nothing. A cigarette-end, lying on a broken ash-tray; a plate with some crumbs on it. He moved about the room, shifting oddments of furniture, eventually looked under the bed.

Something showed up, small and pale.

He fished it out; a small pearl cluster brooch. It was Alice Conway's; she had worn it at the neck of her blouse.

The girl must have been here when he had been talking to Tiger, earlier in the day. He'd told himself that he had come out of that encounter well—and the girl had been lying here, helpless, terrified.

He gritted his teeth.

He heard footsteps coming up the passage, but didn't turn round. He stared at the window, and seemed to see a pair of startling blue eyes—eyes so blue and clear that he couldn't forget them, and knew that he never would.

CHAPTER 19
VITAL NEED

R oss tried to shut out the vision of those blue eyes as he rang the bell at Mae's flat. He couldn't. He had seen Alice Conway for about twenty minutes, certainly not much longer—and he couldn't forget her, he was thinking of her even as he waited for the door to open and before he saw Mae. He wrenched his thoughts away, tried to guess how Mae was now. In bed, probably, with the maid fussing over her.

Mae opened the door.

"Hallo, darling," she said, and drew him inside.

There had been much smart talk between them, the serious moments had been few and far between, and those had been touched by the intensity of passion. That wasn't here now. She was quiet and earnest—she seemed calmer and different. That showed in the way she smiled, the way she spoke, and in the soft touch of her hand. He tried to analyse it as he followed her into the big room, where the chaos had been that morning, but which had been tidied up so that nothing was out of place.

She was more mature.

The cocktail cabinet was open, and she went across and poured out drinks, knowing that he would want whisky. One bar of the electric fire was on, and two arm-chairs were drawn up in front of it; usually, she would have the couch drawn up.

"A long life, darling."

"No more escapades for you," said Ross.

They drank.

Mae sat down; and usually by now she would have flung her arms round him, they would have been losing themselves in the wild joy of passion. He started to sit down, then realised that he hadn't kissed her and hadn't wanted to. He'd brushed her forehead with his lips, at Chancery Lane, that was all. He went across, and stood smiling down.

"All right?"

"Yes, I'm fine, now. He didn't hurt me."

"Wonderful!"

He went down and pressed his lips against hers, but there was something wrong. There wasn't the response that he might have expected, and that was partly due to him. He drew away.

"You must be tired," said Mae. "Sit down, darling."

"I'm not new to this game," he said.

"No, I realise that. I realise a lot of things," said Mae. "It began after you sent me home last night. At first I was— livid." She laughed, lightly, nervously. "To be sent home like a naughty schoolgirl! But that didn't last long, I realised you were really working and there wasn't a blonde—and that I'd been an utter fool. Did you get my note?"

"Yes. Thanks. It's in my pocket."

"I mean what I said."

"I know," said Ross, although he hadn't been and wasn't sure.

"And I've done a lot of thinking since then, I've had time to," said Mae. "If that man's a specimen of the kind you fight, you've plenty to do, and you can't afford to be worrying about the tantrums of a spoiled woman."

"My, my! You'll get introspective."

"It's time I did some thinking," said Mae. "Peter, I don't know what's going to happen between us, I can well understand if you feel that it's all been a mistake. But whatever happens, I shan't be a pest again. You've the job, and I'm not part of it. I wish I could be, but——" She shrugged. "Forget everything I said at the Dive, darling."

"Forgotten," said Peter.

"Can I—help?"

"I doubt it—beyond telling me more about the boy friend," said Ross. "I'm not the boss of the outfit, and agents don't get picked off the nearest tree. You've all the requisites of a bee-ootiful spy, my sweet, but it's tough going."

"Let's be serious," said Mae.

"Did you get any idea of this man's name?"

"None at all."

"What did he talk about?"

Mae said: "That was one of the worst things about it, he said practically nothing after the first interview. He was at the house in the East End, that was the first time I saw him. He wanted to know everything I could tell him about you—especially your work."

"That wasn't much."

"I realised then why you never talked about it," said Mae, and gave an unexpected laugh. "I told him what a brave man you were, testing out these new aeroplanes! After a while, I think he almost believed me!"

Ross grinned.

"I've told all this to one of your colleagues," Mae said. "Loftus sent him along with me—he wanted to stay, and he's in the dining-room now."

"We don't want more trouble for you," said Ross. "Until this is over, you'll be having a paying guest."

Mae shrugged.

He began to see her properly for the first time since he had arrived, was no longer dazzled by bright-blue eyes. She had changed into a black gown of simple cut, with long sleeves and a high neck. She had the figure of a Juno. She had made up lightly, and her hair looked as well as it had done at the Dive. She showed no signs at all of the ordeal, unless it were in dark patches under her eyes, and they were very faint. She showed the effect mostly in her quiet manner, and somehow it wasn't Mae, not the Mae he knew. But she was beautiful, and—desirable.

Her eyes were more grey than green.

"Did you know he searched the flat?" asked Ross.

"Oh, yes, he told me he was going to," said Mae. "And I told him it was a waste of time. Peter, he didn't have it all his own way, I wasn't completely cowed."

Ross chuckled.

"Show me the man who could cow you!"

"You're very sweet," said Mae, and it wasn't the adjective he had expected. "He thought you and I worked together."

"*What?*"

"I told him he was dreaming, but he still thought so. If we didn't, he said, why was I with you last night, why did I follow you? He just wouldn't take no for an answer, that was the only time he tried to frighten me. He made a lot of threats about torture, but didn't carry them out. And while he was making them, I was thinking that if you'd ever told me anything, I'd probably pass it on. I don't think I could stand physical pain. You heard me squeal tonight. I've always—dreaded being hurt. When I was quite young I had an accident in the Welsh mountains, I was there alone for hours and in agony. Since then——"

"I'm not surprised," interrupted Ross. "It isn't a womanly requisite to stand up to that kind of pain, and the boy friend used nice methods."

"I don't know what I'd have done if you hadn't come," said Mae. "Peter, I don't think I shall ever be much good to you."

"Nonsense!"

His voice was louder than he intended it to be.

"Oh, I know you'll say it, but I don't think I shall. In the long run, you'll wish that you had a wife who was more like you. Who could stand the strain of—your work. You can't give that up, I can see that, but you'll need help which I may not be able to give you. I'm—frightened for you. I think subconsciously I've been more worried about you being hurt than about anything else. It was a wonderful time, but——"

He stood up slowly, went across to her, and rested his hands gently on her shoulders, slid them down, and took her hands. They gripped. He pulled her up. They stood very close together, and he could see the flawless beauty of her, felt something of the suffocating wildness of his passion for her.

He kissed her, roughly.

She gasped: "Peter, oh, Peter!"

He kissed her again, and when he stood back, she was breathless, but her eyes were like stars. He felt the wildness in him, but there was something missing—or rather, a something added, a heaviness in his breast, almost a physical thing. He hadn't meant that, had simply put on an act; and Mae had been fooled.

He slid his hand to his waistcoat pocket, and drew out the ring. He tossed it up.

"See that?"

"Peter——"

"It may be your last chance."

She said in an unsteady voice: "Don't unless you're sure, darling."

If he hesitated, she would know the truth, and he sensed that it would hurt her more, perhaps, than she would realise herself. He knew that she would take whatever came with her chin up, but—he couldn't bear to hurt her. He took her hand and slid the ring back on to her finger, kissed it lightly, then kissed her lips.

"Let's make it soon," he said.

"Whenever you like, my darling."

The words were the same, but the vitality wasn't in them. She'd changed; she'd probably changed for the better, but she wasn't the woman whom he had loved.

He left the flat a little after midnight, and drove at once to Whitehall, parked the car in the usual place, then went to Craigie's office. It was second nature to look about him, taking all the usual precautions, but they mocked him. He had taken them when Mae had followed him, had been fooled by an amateur. He was smiling when he stepped into the big room, and saw Craigie sitting back in one of the arm-chairs. No one else was in the office.

"'Lo, Gordon."

"Come and sit down, Peter. A drink?"

"I think I'll give it a miss, thanks." Ross took out cigarettes. "How's business? Anyone else after the air-defence secrets?"

"Not yet!"

"How's Conway?"

"He's much better—he'll be able to leaving the nursing-home in the morning," said Craigie. "He remembers everything, but his story doesn't help us much. It's a simple business, I think, except—we don't know who's behind it. We must find out."

"It shouldn't take long, now—the boy friend can't stay in hiding indefinitely. What about the taxi he got away in?"

"We've found it, but he was dropped near Piccadilly—and he walked all right, couldn't have been too badly hurt. The police are searching Soho, all doctors are being approached to find out if they've attended a man with a gunshot wound, and the hospitals are on the look-out. This is one job where we need police co-operation."

Loftus hadn't been wrong about the police.

"But our man may not be the leader," said Craigie, who talked casually and quietly, and was fiddling with his meer-schaum. "I doubt if he is. Would the big shot of a job like this do so much himself? Who's behind it, Peter? And what else do they want?"

Ross didn't answer.

Craigie said: "I've seen the beginning of a lot of jobs, and when they start like this, they usually finish up in a big way if we can't stop it early. Divide the case into two. First, the Conway side and the air-defence, which is big enough in itself to scare the pundits in Downing Street—you should have heard some of the comments I've had in the past two days! Second—what may follow. They've failed so far with Conway, but they still have his daughter. As soon as he's out of the nursing-home, they may try to have another go at him. He'll be more closely watched, but they'll take every chance they can. We can't be sure what Conway will do if he thinks it's to save his daughter from injury or being killed. There's a wide gap in those defences, and we haven't filled it yet."

Ross said: "I see."

"And there are the other back-room boys. We're having all of them watched," Craigie went on, "and I'm half-expecting to hear that one or two of them have been attacked. I don't think Conway was the beginning or the end of this business. I do think that the setback they've had is making the other side slow down, but the pace might quicken. Don't make any mistake—the missing Alice Conway is the weak link in the chain. Half an hour's talk with Conway could give these people practically everything they want. He probably wouldn't have talked for his own security, but—and it's worth repeating—he might for his daughter's. We'll follow him wherever he goes, but we don't know whom we have to guard against. He could sit on a bus and give the whole game away to anyone with expert knowledge, who only needs to know the key to those air-defence plans to have the whole story. That girl's the pivot on which everything turns, Peter."

"Oh, she's the pivot all right," said Ross. He wanted to change the subject. "Did you find anything at Millicent Street?"

"We haven't found a thing. Tiger led to Bray, Bray led to the unknown. Tiger's part seems pretty self-contained, and he's been killed to make sure he can't talk. I've three men watching Bray, I think there might be an attempt to kill him. If there is, we'll have another lead. We want to be after anything that leads to Alice Conway as fast as we can go. And just as your job was to find Conway and get him out alive, now it's to find his daughter. I'll look after him. And the same conditions apply."

Ross said: "Meaning?"

"You know what I mean."

Ross said slowly: "I suppose I do."

He had to de-humanise himself when he worked for the Department. He had to realise that if Alice Conway were alive and could be hurt, she represented a grave danger. If her father knew she was safe, *or if he knew she was dead*, there need be no fear.

Craigie was telling him the obvious; get Alice Conway, dead or alive.

He stood up.

"Have you let Dolly Leeming go back to Bray?"

"Not yet," said Craigie. "I shan't be able to hold her for long, if Bray starts pressing—and he might, he's hopelessly infatuated with her—he could make a sensation out of this, for wrongful arrest. I don't think we could stand it for long, but we can for another twenty-four hours. What's in your mind?"

"Bray might know a little more," said Ross. "I'll go and see."

CHAPTER 20
QUIET NIGHT

Ross drove to within a hundred yards of Bray's block of flats, and then deliberately walked away from it; he wanted time to think, and he thought best when he was walking. He kept to the side streets, and the night was very quiet, London had been asleep for an hour. Only an occasional car passed him, and as one o'clock struck, he could hear Big Ben and other chimes, few of them striking simultaneously. He knew that he was not being followed, and yet stopped at most corners to look round.

The unknown was on the run, but Craigie was obviously right, that man wasn't the leader.

Who was?

How much did he know but hadn't recognised yet?

There were puzzling features, and he had been too preoccupied to try to sort them out. No doubt Craigie and Loftus were doing that, but they couldn't know everything he did—the little, obscure things which seemed to have no significance, but which were important when seen in their proper perspective. One factor running constantly through the affair was different from anything he had met before. Practically without exception, each discovery was complete in itself; or seemed to be.

He'd got to Tiger, and that was as far as he could get. It had been the same with Bray. Conway had flared up as the supremely important objective, but that was no longer true of him. Even Mae had loomed very large at one time—but everything that had happened to her had been explained neatly and logically.

Ah!

Everything was too neat and logical, that was what he was trying to tell himself.

Tiger was just a bad man who had twisted and turned—and got himself killed. Bray had started off with some piece of crookedness, and laid himself open to blackmail, and the explanation had seemed perfectly satisfactory, so much that it almost stifled further investigation; it shouldn't have done, but it had—because it fitted in with the pattern like everything that had occurred.

Now, it was simply a question of finding a girl with startlingly blue eyes—alive or dead.

Craigie had put his finger on the facts with ruthless logic. It wasn't the kind of job Ross had envisaged when he had joined the Department, but he could see its importance. Work for the Department was like working in a kind of home-made hell. He had to squeeze the humanity out of himself, and that was also logical—no man who allowed his ordinary human emotions free rein could serve the Department as it had to be served.

Harry Marshall and Brown had served; and died.

But he wasn't to work because of the hatred he felt towards their killers. Their deaths had been incidental to the main issue. Brown would go in Craigie's little black book and be marked Number 118. The coldness of it was the worst factor.

Now, coldly and deliberately, he had to find the way to Alice Conway, and if he couldn't rescue her alive, had to make sure that she died.

He neared the big block of flats. A car passed and pulled up outside it, and a man and a woman in evening-dress got out and were saluted by the night-porter; their chauffeur drove the car away.

He mustn't forget the risk—that because so much was logical and fully explained, some things might not be. He had a feeling—Loftus would call it a hunch—that he had missed something which was so obvious he would be aghast when he realised what he'd done.

Was it with Bray?

Bray's story had been convincing, and Bray had led him to the mystery man, which had seemed thoroughly satisfactory. Was it?

The porter wasn't alone; one of Craigie's men was sitting at a table, glancing through glossy magazines. He looked up, incuriously, and showed no sign that he recognised Ross.

"Good evening, sir," greeted the porter.

"I'm going to see Mr. Bray."

"Second floor, sir, I'll take you up."

"Thanks."

Another of Craigie's men was at the second floor landing, sitting in an easy-chair which commanded a view of the front door of Bray's flat. He winked. Department Z men were everywhere—surely Conway could be fully protected, now.

Alice *was* the weak link.

Ross went along the passage, but returned when the lift had taken the porter down.

"Has he been out and about?"

"Not lately," said the agent. "His man came in an hour ago—we'd tailed him, and Craigie knows where he'd been. No other visitors." The agent was a young, willowy man, who had not been long in the Department's service. "Any hope?"

"Of what?"

"Fun and games," said the other, promptly.

Ross forced a grin.

"There's always hope," he said.

He knew that most of the others found flippancy and facetiousness an aid to the work—it stopped them from becoming too tense. Probably it would be a good thing if he could feel flippant, too, but he certainly didn't as he rang the bell at Bray's flat.

Bray's man, tall, elderly, and obsequious, opened the door.

"Good evening, sir."

It was now ten past one in the morning; late for a man to be on duty.

"Tell Mr. Bray I've called, will you? Ross."

"Very good, sir."

Watson went off in stately fashion across the hall, and Ross followed swift and silent, so that he could look into the big room. Watson stepped just inside. Bray was sitting back in a deep arm-chair, and smoking a cigar.

"Mr. Ross has called, sir."

"Ross? Oh, *Ross*," repeated Bray, and sighed. "Show him in, Watson, show him in at once. Any time Mr. Ross calls, I'll be glad to see him."

Watson turned, as Ross backed away. The man did not seem surprised to see his visitor so close. The absurd formality was continued.

"Mr. Bray will see you, sir."

"Thanks," said Ross.

He went in and waited until the door closed. Bray was standing up now, cigar in his hand. He looked tired and rather flabby. He wore the same suit that he had earlier in the evening, and there was almost pathetic eagerness in his expression as he spoke. Ross watched him closely, trying to judge whether what he said was the truth or a lie, trying to find out whether this man had deeper qualities than anyone yet suspected.

"I kept *my* part of the bargain, Ross," said Bray.

"Yes, I know."

"And"—Bray's eyes almost glowed—"did you *find* the man?"

"He escaped."

Bray said: "Oh, no! No, you shouldn't have let him do that." He sat down abruptly, his colour faded. "Ross, that was a terrible mistake, terrible, because he may know I led him into a trap. Oh, Ross!"

"Has he been in touch with you?"

Bray said: "Of course he hasn't. But he may try, now."

"Why so scared?"

"I think you should know," said Bray. "That man has always alarmed me, I have always felt that there was great capacity for evil in him. Do you mean to tell me—you didn't—find *Mae?*"

Ross kept silent.

"But there's nothing more I can do," protested Bray. "*I* did my share, it was your own folly to let the man go. You can't expect me to do anything more."

"What else can you do?"

"Nothing! That's the whole point, I've done my level best, and gave you a chance at great risk to myself—and you've thrown that chance away. Now—Dolly——"

He broke off.

"Poor Dolly," said Ross.

Bray sat back and looked at him, put the cigar to his mouth, took it away again, and then stood up. Every movement was slow and considered, and, as once before, he assumed a kind of dignity; it was easy to smile at it, but the dignity was there. He walked towards Ross, and peered up at him; he looked very tired.

"Where is Miss Leeming?"

"We'll talk business when——"

"You will release Miss Leeming forthwith, or I shall complain first to Scotland Yard and then, if necessary, to the Home Secretary's Private Parliamentary Secretary," said Bray, uttering the words with great care. "I shall, if necessary, carry the matter to the highest possible authority. I know that you have some authority yourself, I am not deceived, but by these means you are exceeding it. I hope you understand me, Ross. If you release Miss Leeming now, I shall say nothing about it, but failing that——"

He glanced at the telephone.

"I'm nervous," said Ross.

"You have cause to be. Let me remind you that the Press of this country is always watchful in the interests of the freedom of the citizen. In a matter of this kind several of the big newspapers would be only too ready to take up an abuse of authority, and I know several influential men in Fleet Street. I shall fight, Ross—no matter how strong your hand nor how great your own authority, and I do not think that would be a good thing for you."

"Don't you?"

Bray cried: "Don't stand there leering at me and uttering cryptic comments on everything I say. I'm not a fool! I know the risks, but you can't blackmail me. *He* has, and I've suffered for it, and I'll suffer more, but I will *not* allow Miss Leeming to suffer. Do you understand? Release her!"

Ross said quietly: "Supposing you calm down?"

He went across to a chair and sat down, and Bray looked at him as if surprised by the sudden moderation in his tone. Ross lit a cigarette, and glanced meaningly at the whisky bottle by the side of Bray's chair. Bray didn't make a move towards it, but his temper evaporated.

"I hope I've made myself clear."

"Very clear. I've also told you that this is a murder case. Your friend killed again, tonight, while getting away. I don't think you've told me everything you know about him."

"But I have!"

"How did you get in touch with him for tonight's meeting?" asked Ross softly.

"He telephoned me! I had no idea how to get in touch with him, but he frequently gets me on the telephone. I told him that I had to see him, and he reluctantly agreed to meet me in Regent Street. I made the excuse that your visit had frightened me——"

"Excuse?"

"Very well," said Bray, "it was no excuse. You have scared me, because of Miss Leeming. But don't make any mistake, unless she is freed at once I shall take steps to make sure that the newspapers have this story in the morning. They may smear me with mud, but they won't harm Dolly. I will give you——" He glanced at a gold Regency clock on the wall, pursed his lips, and went on: "Precisely one and a half hours."

"Thanks," said Ross. "What did the man look like?"

"It was dark, and——"

"They have lights in Regent Street."

"He wore a cap pulled low over his eyes and kept the collar of his coat turned up," Bray said wearily. "His eyes were almost all I could see, and his long nose. Oh, and his hair was fair at the back—blond."

"Well, well," breathed Ross. "What good eyes you have, grandpa! A long nose and fair hair—are you sure about that?"

"I will not be insulted!"

"Still sure?"

Bray licked his lips and backed away, saw the whisky and hurried across to it, picking it up and then looking round as if for another glass. He started towards the cocktail cabinet, bottle in hand, but Ross caught his arm and made him stop. He didn't try to free himself.

"The man had dark hair and a short nose," said Ross. "I know that. Now let's really start talking business!"

Chapter 21
New Lead

"He—he didn't look like that to me," Bray gasped, and stood helpless in Ross's grip. "I told you there wasn't much light, and there was only the hair at the back of his head. I thought——"

"You wouldn't think a short nose was a long one or dark hair was fair, in the lights of Regent Street." Ross pressed the little man's wrist tightly, making Bray wince, then let him go and backed away. "Don't let us get excited, Bray. Why are you trying to tell me that he's different? Hoping that I'll tell the police to send out the wrong description."

"My—my eyes aren't good in the dark," Bray muttered. "Ask anybody—ask my chauffeur, I never drive at night because of my eyes. And I couldn't see the man well, that's the truth. He—he may have been disguised."

"Well, what a bright idea," said Ross.

It might be true. A false nose and a wig might pass, at night, provided there was no close scrutiny; there had been neither nose nor wig at the Chancery Lane Offices, but the man might have slipped them into his pocket. Bray was an odd mixture; he didn't strike a note of confidence, he was wriggling and frightened, yet he didn't seem to Ross to be lying. He was too earnest.

"It must be true!" muttered Bray.

"We'll see. I want this man, and I think you can tell me where to find him."

"I can't!"

"Poor Dolly."

Bray backed away, picked up his whisky-glass, and again took on that unlikely appearance of dignity. He didn't speak for some seconds, seemed to be getting himself under strict control. Twice he started to speak, only to stop; finally, he cleared his throat and said huskily:

"I have no more time for you. I've delivered my ultimatum. You know what I shall do if Dolly hasn't come here within the next—the next one and a *quarter* hours." He raised his head challengingly, expecting comment on the lost quarter of an hour.

"But you'll be detained yourself."

"I shall ask for my lawyer."

"You have all the answers, except the one I want most," said Ross. He was favourably impressed by the man's manner, and relaxed again; but Bray didn't relax, and looked pointedly at the clock. Ross ignored his glance. "Bray, you say this man often telephones you and that he called you again tonight. Did he always speak from the same number?"

"*I* don't know."

"Are you sure you've never seen him before?"

"Of course I'm sure."

"Although he blackmailed you, you made no attempt to find out who he was."

"How could I? I could have gone to the police, and that would have meant telling them the whole story. I had no desire to tell the police about my past, I was prepared to pay for the man's silence."

"Chiefly because it didn't cost you much, I fancy. And you never got a line on him."

"No, never. There was one time when I was hopeful, but the trail petered out."

"What trail?"

"I hope you realise that your time is passing," said Bray, and managed to sound frigid. "It was at the Dive—I received a note there. One of the demands, framed in similar phrases to the telephone calls, and I tried to find out who'd sent it to me. No one seemed to know, the waiters and the barman said they'd no idea. Apparently the note had been left on a table with my name on the envelope. That's all."

"Well, well," breathed Ross. "The Dive again."

Bray didn't speak.

Ross stood up.

"Listen to me, Sammy. You're in deep waters, and there's a lot at stake. You may know it. If you don't, I can tell you this much—no one is going to stop doing anything because you've friends in high places. Dolly will be all right, if you're on the level, but if you start trying to work up Press indignation you'll have some nasty surprises. Any other leads to this mystery man?"

"No."

Bray licked his lips.

"What did he look like?"

Bray said wearily: "It's no use trying to trick me. I *thought* he had a long nose and fair hair, that's the most I can say. I'm not impressed by your threats. I may have made a fool of myself in the past, but I'm a wealthy man now, and I'm not dishonest *or* disloyal. If you'd approached me in the right way, I would gladly have cooperated."

"All right, Sammy," said Ross. "Perhaps I've misjudged you."

He went out swiftly; Bray hardly realised he had gone when he closed the door. He hurried along the passage, and was stopped by the hopeful young agent, who said promptly:

"Anything?"

"Not yet." Ross took out cigarettes. "Is his telephone line tapped, do you know?"

"Oh, yes—Hope is watching the switchboard, downstairs."

"Thanks." Ross lit both their cigarettes and hurried on, beckoned the man who was still sitting at the table and reading a glossy magazine. The porter was in his office, where a switchboard was built into the wall. "Hope, he may try to make some calls, and one of them might be to the Dive. He hasn't called anyone tonight yet, has he?"

"Not since I was on duty," said Hope, a fair-haired, blue-eyed man. The light shone into his eyes, and Ross frowned, for no apparent reason at all. "I'll make sure Craigie hears if there's anything. Any message from you, if he rings up?"

"Just that I've gone to the Dive."

Everything about Bray had started at the Dive; he'd first hit the trail there. It was open until two-thirty, providing music and dancing. He wished he hadn't left his car so far away. He hurried towards it, slid into the driving seat, and switched on the engine.

As he leaned forward to release the handbrake, he heard a rustle of movement in the back seat, but wasn't able to do anything to save himself. A blow smashed on to the back of his head, crushing his hat; another sent him lurching over the wheel. The engine stalled. He didn't shout, just grunted and waited for the next blow.

He couldn't move.

He heard vague sounds, and the third blow came, but it wasn't heavy, and it struck him on the shoulder. He heard more sounds, as of voices, and then the wind blew in and he knew that the door had opened. He heard a louder shout, then the bark of a shot. At this, he tried to straighten up, but his head was burning with pain, he had hardly the wit to feel relieved. The sound of voices stopped, and there was no more shooting, but there were footsteps—and then a police whistle shrilled out.

He was doing well with the police.

A man spoke close to his ear.

"Peter—sit up!"

It was Williamson, tense with alarm.

Ross grunted.

Williamson took Ross's hat off, then switched on the courtesy light in the roof. It seemed so bright that it hurt Ross's eyes, and he grunted again. He felt Williamson's fingers probing, and winced twice when the man touched a tender spot, but he was already feeling better; the sickness of fear and of pain were receding. Williamson pushed him away from the wheel, and leaned him back.

"All ri'," he muttered. "Give me—five minutes."

Another man spoke in the deep, formal voice he associated with policemen. Williamson got out, but left the door open. Ross didn't try to follow the conversation, but straightened up, and took in long, deep breaths of air. Soon he was much better, apart from the ache in his head.

Williamson came back.

"I'll drive you home."

"No—the Dive."

"Not in those trousers, old chap."

"Don't be a fool. The Dive."

"So you've found something," said Williamson.

"I might find a needle in that haystack." Talking was painful because it jarred the muscles at the back of his head, but Ross went on: "What happened?"

"The swine was lying in wait for you, and I was too far away. I got him, though."

"*What?*"

Williamson was grim.

"I got him too well, I doubt if he'll come through. Pity— he would have talked, I think. Nothing special about him, he looks just a tough. Tell me what you want to find out at the Dive, and I'll see what I can do."

Ross forced a smile.

"Don't think I don't trust you, but you don't know Sam."

"We'll look in at your flat first," said Williamson.

Ross put his head under the cold tap, and Williamson held it under. Ross gasped, but didn't try to back away. Williamson put a towel round his head, when the dowsing was done, and he staggered to the bathroom stool. Williamson dabbed his hair gently, and Ross took the towel and rubbed vigorously; it hurt, but it didn't take so long. Then he went into his living-room, and gave Williamson a whisky, and himself two aspirins. His eyes were bloodshot, but apart from that he was feeling much more himself. It was still nearly an hour to the time the Dive closed.

Williamson drove.

"I'm getting used to a chauffeur," said Ross.

"Get used to thinking. They want you pretty badly, Peter."

"Why any worse now?"

"Well, they want you—it's as well Craigie had a notion that they might, and gave me the job of following you round."

"I need following round," said Ross.

His mind wasn't fit for much thinking, but the fact sunk in that there had been a deliberate attempt to kill him—and that could only be because of what he knew. What *did* he know? What would justify their taking the risk of hiring a man to kill him? It was someone who was watching pretty closely, and who guessed that he would be back at Bray's. Was it something which he had discovered at Bray's—or what the attacker might think he had discovered?

Williamson pulled up, near the Dive.

"Not many cars about tonight, it'll be nearly empty," he said. "Sure you won't let me ask the questions?"

"Just be a watchdog," pleaded Ross.

Williamson chuckled.

Ross went past the respectful commissionaire and down the carpeted steps. He heard a mutter of voices, and Sam's "Yes, sah!" uttered in a way which suggested that whoever he was talking to was the only man worth any attention; Sam had a genius for making his clients seem important. The lights were bright, but didn't hurt Ross's eyes. Inside the Dive itself the lighting was much more sub-dued. There were about a dozen people there, and Sam was leaning against the bar, talking to a middle-aged man who was propping himself up with his elbows and speaking in a slurred voice; he seemed likely to fall asleep at any moment.

Sam's eyes flashed round towards the door, and he grinned broadly.

"Pardon me, sah." He left the drunk and came along the bar, still grinning. "Glad to see you, Massa Ross, I've almost forgotten what yo' looked like, sah!"

"What, a man with a memory like yours?" asked Ross.

Sam's grin nearly split his face in two.

"That all depends, sah. For some things my memory's wonderful, yes, sah, I'll say it's wonderful, and for other things—believe me, Massa Ross, for other things it seems to me I forget them as if they never happened! What will you have to drink tonight, sah?"

"A tonic water."

Sam's smile faded.

"You feeling okay, Massa Ross?"

"No, Sam." Ross glanced round. No one was near; the others were gathered in one corner in a noisy group, and the drunk was muttering to himself. "You remember Mr. Bray?"

"Sho' do, sah."

"Some time ago, he was worried because someone left him a message, and he didn't know who it came from. Remember?"

"Sho' do. Most upset, Mr. Bray was that night, I never seen him so upset."

So Bray hadn't lied about that.

"Did you do everything you could to help him, Sam?"

"Sho' I did," said Sam, nodding portentously. "I spoke to every waiter, and some of the customers, sah, but no one could remember how that note got on to that table, no, sah! It was a mighty funny thing. I knew the person who had been sitting there, and asked him—no, sah, he hadn't sent no note to Mr. Bray. I did everything a man could do, sah, I would have helped if there'd been any way to help. But there just wasn't any way."

Ross said slowly: "That's a great pity, Sam. What table was it on?"

Sam pointed a knuckly forefinger.

"Right there—right under my eyes. I looked up and saw it and thought some gennulman had left a letter behind, and then I saw it was addressed to Mr. Bray, sah, so I took it right to him. He was very upset, I haven't often seen a gennulman so upset."

"And you can't remember anything else, with that wonderful memory of yours, Sam?"

"Not a dam' thing," declared Sam, and had never smiled more brightly.

"Sam," said Ross to himself, "I don't believe you."

But he didn't say it aloud.

CHAPTER 22
BACK ROOM

Ross sipped his tonic water and watched Sam serving the party in the corner, and wondered if he were crazy. The Dive would be a good cover for any form of crime—was so obvious that it was too obvious. There wasn't much evidence—just the fact that Sam had put him on to Bray, and Sam wasn't telling the truth now. He didn't know Sam well, but had had much to do with his race. Sam was uneasy, and the only likely reason was because he was lying.

That could spring from fear, because he knew who had sent the letter to Bray but had been coerced into lying. Sam might be able to give another lead which would point away from the Dive; or the Dive might be the hub of the organisation.

Sam came back.

"Yo' sho' look as if you have a bad head, Massa Ross, yo' ought to go home and have some sleep."

"I'm thinking just that, Sam."

"Yo'll be better in the morning, sah," said Sam. "I confess I've been thinking mighty hard about that letter and Mr. Bray, but I just can't remember a thing that would be of assistance. I can't tell you how sorry I am, Massa Ross."

"You've been wonderful, Sam. Forget it."

"That's just what I have done, sah!" But Sam didn't grin with the sally; he was serious; and that meant he was agitated.

Ross looked round at the others, recognised two or three of them, and wondered if they were involved. He grinned to himself as he turned away, nodding to Sam; if he went on like this he would think everyone who ever entered the Dive was mixed up in the mystery of the men who wanted the atomic air-defence plans.

It was good to breathe the crisp air of the night.

Williamson loomed up, out of dark shadows.

"Now it's time for shut-eye, Peter."

"Not yet, old chap. I'm going to see Craigie."

"He'll love that, at this hour. Want me?"

Ross hesitated, and said: "I don't know who sleeps on the premises, Tim. Keep an eye open, if any of the staff leave make a note of their names, and if anyone goes in and doesn't leave at throwing-out time, we may be interested."

"Now what's this?" asked Williamson, heavily.

"Things not being what they seem—the usual grind."

Ross went off, got into his car, and turned to look into the back seat. It wasn't until now that the delayed-action effect of the attack hit at his nerves, and that was partly because his head wasn't too good. He crashed his gears as he changed up, and hadn't done that for a long time. He sped through the quiet streets and half-expected a chase car or shots out of the darkness.

Why had he been attacked? Forget it.

He knew that Craigie or Loftus would be at the office; built into the wall there was a bed, which could be lowered.

But there was no delay after he had pressed the switch, the doors opened and Loftus bulked against the light. Several of the lamps were turned off, and Craigie was lying in the bed, not far from the fireplace. He was wide awake, and a book was lying on the sheet. Loftus was fully dressed.

"Sorry about this," said Ross, "but I'm full of ideas."

"We need them," said Loftus.

Ross explained briefly, and his arguments didn't seem so strong when he was talking to the others as when he had only himself for an audience; it hadn't seemed overpowering, even then. He watched the faces of the Department leaders, both sober and serious—and knew just how deeply this affair was affecting them. They couldn't see the end yet.

Need they be worried? The other side seemed to be on the run.

"And that's it," he said at last. "Tell me I ought to go and sleep it off."

"You probably think better when you think you can't think at all," said Loftus with heavy humour. "We've just had a message from Berry, who had a crack at the man Tim shot. Your assailant. The man isn't dead, but he isn't far off it—and he's talked. He had to kidnap you, if he could."

"Nice," said Ross.

"If it had worked the way he planned, he would have knocked you out and then driven you to Hyde Park Corner, where another man would have taken over the car. He doesn't know your final destination, but he does know where he got his orders."

Ross didn't speak.

"From a man at the Dive," said Loftus. "He met the man outside there, two hours before he attacked you. We've laid on men for a raid—our chaps this time, not the police. It's due at a quarter to three, when the last of the ordinary members should have left. Coming?"

The little neon sign outside the front door of the Dive went out as Ross and Williamson took up their positions in a shadowy doorway, farther along the narrow street. The commissionaire was visible against the inside light, and was obviously waiting for someone to come out. Two couples, one man the worse for drink, left a few minutes afterwards; the commissionaire's thanks for a substantial tip floated along the road. Under cover of the noise of the car engines starting up, Ross and Williamson went forward and other Department agents closed in. There was only the one entrance, as far as anyone knew, but agents were also watching the buildings at the back of the Dive; there might be a secret exit.

Ross reached the door as the commissionaire was closing it.

"Hallo," said Ross. "Too late?"

"I'm afraid you are, sir."

"I left my cigarette-case downstairs."

"Oh, you can go and get that," said the commissionaire. "I'm in no hurry. Empty earlier to-night than usual."

He nodded affably as Ross and Williamson went down, then looked in surprise at the others.

Ross didn't worry about the commissionaire.

He led the way slowly down the stairs and past the empty cloaks cubicle. The cloakroom attendant wasn't there, but he heard a woman laughing inside, and, at the door, saw the attendant with a glass at her lips, looking at Sam, who leaned across the bar as if well satisfied with the night's work and prepared to go on talking for a long time. The other barmen were tidying up, and from a little room behind the bar there came the chink of glasses being washed.

Ross slipped into the room.

Sam started, recognised him, and stared, his mouth dropping wide open, his eyes nearly popping out of his head. The woman looked puzzled but not alarmed. Ross grinned and approached the bar, his right hand in his pocket—and then Sam turned and bolted through the narrow doorway which led to the kitchen.

Ross put a hand on the bar and vaulted over, snatching up a bottle of gin.

Sam shouted to someone unseen.

Ross reached the little wash-room, and saw another door open and Sam disappearing. He flung the bottle and caught Sam on the back of the head, pitching the man forward— Sam seemed to fall on his face and his legs kicked. There was a scuffling sound in the room beyond. Ross reached the doorway, gun in hand now, and saw two men in a room not more than ten feet by ten. Sam had banged his head on the desk behind which one of the men was standing.

The other was by his side—also gun in hand.

Ross fired. His bullet struck the other's gun and knocked it from his grasp. The man by the desk grabbed at something in an open drawer. Ross snapped:

"Keep away."

The man hesitated.

"Show your hands," said Ross.

Slowly, the man withdrew his hands. Ross went across and plucked another automatic from the drawer. It had come so swiftly that it almost surprised him. There seemed to be no other way out of the room, the walls were cream distempered and quite blank. There were two arm-chairs and two upright chairs, the desk, a corner cupboard, a small table, and two telephones—that was all.

Sam was gasping, and trying to get up.

Williamson came in, and drawled:

"They don't seem pleased to see you, Peter."

"They aren't pleased," said Ross, "but they may get a laugh later on."

Sam got to his knees and crawled on all fours to a chair, then sat on the floor with his back against the chair and his chin on his chest. Williamson went across and frisked him; Sam didn't carry a weapon.

Ross studied the two men.

He had seen them both before, and knew one of them by name—a medium-sized man who was running to fat. He had broad features and the rather weak eyes behind thick-lensed glasses. His hair was quite grey, but he had plenty of it, and also had the indefinable look of the north country-man. He was Higson, the owner of the Dive.

The other man was taller, dressed in evening clothes, and was younger. He was often here, usually with a woman. He was pale and scared, and that had shaken out of him any claim to good looks.

The only man who didn't show fear was Higson.

"You stand in that corner, you in that."

Ross jerked the gun towards the respective corners, and the younger man obeyed at once. Higson hesitated. Williamson crossed to him, and took his arm, and Higson didn't resist. When they were in their respective corners, Williamson backed to the door and took out his gun. The other raiding agents poked their heads in.

"Having a nice time?" That was Perry, who looked like a whippet.

"Wonderful," said Ross. "Have a good look round every-where, won't you?"

He went to the desk and sat down, then opened all the drawers and took out the contents—and suddenly he stopped. He drew out a wig—a man's wig of blond hair. Next, he took out a false nose, long and wriggly. He nodded with satisfaction and held the wig up.

"Yours, Higson?"

Higson didn't speak.

"Or your wounded boy friend's," said Ross.

He glanced through the papers and saw little of interest, until he came to a packet of photographs. He shook these out and spread them on the desk. Mae was there; Conway; Alice Conway...

He found himself staring at Alice; and putting blue in place of the grey in the photograph. He put that aside quickly. There was a photograph of himself—a good one. He had never seen it before, had no idea where it had been taken. Bray, Dolly Leeming, several other agents—but neither Loftus nor Craigie—were there. Also, there were pictures of the three men who had died at the house at Shepperton.

That raid seemed an age ago.

He finished looking through them.

"Nice picture gallery," he said. "Why don't you like your picture taken, Higson?"

Higson didn't speak. Neither of the men had uttered a word since the raid.

Ross turned the photographs over, and on the back was a potted biography. His own name, address, and approximate age were noted down, and there was a note: *"Independent means; believed Intelligence agent."*

"How did you get the wig and false nose?" Ross asked mildly.

Higson didn't speak; the man in evening clothes licked his lips and stared at Higson, as if ready to take his cue from the north countryman. It was Sam who stirred, got to his feet unsteadily, and looked at Ross with his mouth hanging open and a scared glow in his dark eyes.

"Massa Ross, sah, they was brung in, early to-night."

"Who brought them?"

"A man from outside, sah."

Higson said in a thin, cruel voice: "Now keep your mouth shut, Sam, or you'll suffer for it."

"Shut up," Ross barked. "Go on, Sam."

"They was just brung in," said Sam. "A little guy said that they had finished with them, sah. Also——"

"Keep your mouth shut!" Higson snarled.

Sam darted a sideways look at him.

"There was one other thing, Massa Ross, sah. The man who brung them said that there had been some trouble and that Elliott was wounded, sah, that's God's truth. I didn't imagine it, Massa Ross, he said Elliott was wounded."

"Elliott," mused Ross. "Do you know Elliott?"

"Sure thing, sah! He's often been here, he——"

The roar of a shot cut across his words.

It didn't come from Higson or the tall man—but from the wall, near the corner cupboard. Sam choked. Ross saw him stagger, saw the wound on his forehead. Sam was dead before he hit the floor. Higson rushed towards the cupboard, the doors of which were open. Williamson shot him in the leg and brought him down. The younger man, farther away from the corner, groaned but didn't move. Ross went quickly to the cupboard, knowing another shot might come at any moment. There was darkness beyond a hole in the wall, a sound of footsteps but no more shooting.

"Careful!" cried Williamson.

Ross went into the cupboard and through the hole in the wall, knowing he was a clear target against the light of the office.

CHAPTER 23
ELLIOTT

O ut of sight, a door slammed.

Ross could see from the light behind him. He was in a narrow passage, and there seemed to be a door at the far end. Immediate danger was gone. He kept one hand against the wall and hurried along, and footsteps told him that Williamson or Perry was behind him. Probably Perry— the passage was low, and Williamson would have difficulty getting along it.

He reached the door.

There was a handle, and it was an ordinary wooden door. He turned the handle and pushed, and was surprised that the door wasn't locked. A faint light came from ahead of him. He stepped through cautiously into a large office, with several desks and typewriters, filing-cabinets and telephones.

Perry called out from behind him.

"Found the switch, Peter?"

The light ahead went out almost on his words, and another door slammed. But this would lead into the streets at the back of the Dive, and agents were watching. It should be a complete haul. Ross thought: "And Alice?" and wondered what he would feel if he found her, then cursed himself for thinking of it.

He reached the far wall as Perry switched on a torch. The beam caught the electric-light switch, and Ross pressed it down.

Bright light flooded the office, which looked smaller now. Cigarette smoke curled up from two ash-trays. It looked as if several people had been in here when the alarm had been raised. Ross went to the door, and found it locked.

He shot twice at the lock.

He stood aside, and Perry took a chance and went ahead of him into a narrow passage which led to a flight of stairs. There were no sounds now—but that didn't mean the danger was gone. Perry went up the stairs at the double. At the top was another door, and he fired at this lock before thrusting it open. This time Ross went through first.

He was in a bedroom.

A man lay on a single bed, eyes open, right arm and shoulder bandaged. He was groping for something beneath his pillow with his good hand. Ross went across and gripped his wrist, then slid his own hand beneath the pillow and drew out an automatic.

"Where have they gone?" he asked.

The man on the bed didn't speak.

"You might as well save us time, Elliott, that's all that's in it."

"Go to hell," muttered Elliott.

He had dark hair, a short nose, and brown eyes; and it was easy to imagine that the hatred smouldering in those eyes could frighten—as they had frightened Mae. He looked sinewy and powerful, and there wasn't any doubt that he was the man whom Bray had meant, and whom Ross had wounded. His lips were thin and drawn back now; it might have been in pain or in hatred. There wasn't any doubt about his hatred, either—he looked a fanatic.

Ross said: "Where's Alice Conway?"

"You'll never catch up, you fool."

Ross went across to the far door. It wasn't locked, and led to a sitting-room. This was a small flat, nicely furnished; he judged that several people lived here. He crossed the sitting-room to a small hall, then opened the front door. He was in a small mews, and knew that it was immediately behind the Dive. He could see no one in the mews, and that puzzled him; the other agents ought to be here.

He called out: "Hallo, there!"

There was no answer.

Perry joined him.

"We keep chasing shadows," he complained.

"Keep an eye on Elliott, will you?"

"No need—Tim's there."

"All right," said Ross. A flight of steps led down into the mews, and he went down cautiously, then realised that it was very dark. The street lights were out. In corners, the darkness was pitch, and the only light came from the stairs and the door from which Ross had come. He said: "Torch, old chap?"

The torch shone out, the long beam stabbing right and left—until suddenly it stopped. It showed a man's face—and the man was lying on his back. Perry hurried across to him, and before Ross had moved, called out:

"It's Parkson."

Parkson was one of the Department agents.

"Just K.O.'d.," Perry called with relief in his voice.

He swivelled the torch round again, and they saw a second man lying in another corner. He was more badly hurt than Parkson—there was blood on his collar and shirt, and a wound in his cheek; but he was alive.

"They were ready for us, Peter."

It hardly needed conscious thought to see what had happened. The gang had been alive to trouble, had discovered they were being watched and knew that agents were stationed in the mews; and they had sent for others, from outside, to attack the watching men and so make sure that they could escape. It wasn't any good wasting time or wishing for the moon. For a few moments he had thought that this was the end of the chase, but he'd simply driven them from one hole to another—and had caught some of the rats.

A car came along the road approaching the mews, headlights full on. It stopped, the headlights stayed on, and footsteps approached. The new-comer was Loftus, hurrying and limping badly.

"No Alice," said Ross. "Another dead end."

Ross woke up at half past ten next morning, and wondered why he had a headache—until he remembered what had happened. There was plenty to remember. He sat up and felt his head; it was very tender, and not surprising that it ached. He pushed back the bedclothes, switched on the electric kettle in the fireplace, and went to the bathroom. His eyes were bloodshot, and his face was unusually pale. He grinned at himself, to make sure that he could still look cheerful.

He took the morning newspapers from the letter-box, and skimmed through them; there was a report of the shooting at Chancery Lane and an almost entirely guess-work story of what had led up to it. That was all. He tossed the papers aside, made tea, and smoked a cigarette while sitting on the side of the bed and calling his thoughts to order.

He had left Loftus and other agents at the offices and the flat behind the Dive—Loftus had given him orders to come here, and he hadn't argued. Loftus was the man for searching and routine, he was simply a man of action—paid to get results. Every time he thought he had them, he found that more results were waiting—out of sight.

Elliott and Higson hadn't said a useful word.

The man in evening dress hadn't appeared to know much more than that the secret entrance to the flat was used by Higson. Sam hadn't even known about it.

He had been in Higson's pay for a sound reason—he was in the country on a forged passport; Higson knew that. He had taken messages which had been brought to the Dive, and done exactly what Higson had told him. He'd given Bray away because he had not known Bray was connected in any way with the case. Making Ross consider Bray had seemed a brilliant diversion.

Ross didn't know what had been discovered at the cellar office; he only knew that they had uncovered part of a sizeable organisation. It was even possible that the results were better than he realised, it might simply be a question of clearing up the odds and ends, but one thing remained—to find Alice Conway.

Why did they want her?

Was Craigie right? Just so that they could exert pressure on her father?

What was the use of guessing?

He poured himself out another cup of tea. The daily woman had been told not to come in for a few days—he preferred to be on his own at a time like this. He went to the dressing-table mirror. He needed a shave badly, and he hadn't improved since he had last looked at his reflection. He swallowed the tea quickly and went to the telephone.

Craigie was in the office, and answered promptly.

"How's the Professor?" asked Ross.

"Going home today—and he'll be closely watched, don't worry."

"No one's tried to get at him at the nursing-home, about Alice?"

"No."

"Thanks," said Ross.

He was on the way to the bathroom when the front-door bell rang. He hesitated.

He went back into the bedroom, took a gun from the chair by the bed and slipped it into his dressing-gown pocket, then went along and opened the door, standing to one side, prepared for anything; if they'd tried to kill once, they would again.

"Hallo, Peter," said Mae.

"Well, well," said Ross, "you've caught me at my best." He drew aside, and Mae came in. "Verbal salutations only, I'm not respectable enough to be kissed."

"You're no worse than I was last night."

"Don't you believe it. How are you? Evil memories gone?"

"Not yet." She peered into his eyes. "What happened to you, after you left me?"

"A thoughtless tough hit me over the head, I wasn't drinking too much," said Ross. "And he didn't last long, Williamson was acting as my bodyguard. See how important I am—I have people to make sure I don't run into trouble."

"I don't think anything could stop you from running into trouble," said Mae.

She went straight into the kitchen. Occasionally they had spent the evening here, and she had cooked an omelette and prepared a light supper.

"Had breakfast?"

Her voice was casual.

"Not yet, and it's nearly lunch-time."

"I'll get you something," said Mae. "You go and shave."

He went into the bathroom and ran the bath; he had seldom bathed and shaved so quickly. Twenty minutes later, fully dressed, he went into the kitchen and found Mae with one of the daily woman's aprons round her beige-coloured suit, frying eggs. Her hair was a little untidy, and she was flushed from the heat of the gas-stove. She looked almost gay. As her left hand moved, the sun which shone through a corner of the kitchen window glinted on the great diamond of the engagement ring. Ross looked away from it.

"Domestic bliss, preview thereof! Can I help?"

"I've laid the table," said Mae. "Do you mind company for breakfast?"

"Shape of things to come!"

They carried bacon and eggs, coffee and toast into the living-room, where she had laid a table in the window. He didn't know why this evidence of Mae's domesticity puzzled him, he'd seen it before. It was largely because he knew she hadn't yet explained why she had come. She remained gay, it was a good half-hour until they were drinking the second cup of coffee and smoking cigarettes.

"How do I look now I'm fed?"

"You look all right," said Mae; "a knock over the head won't hurt you, provided nothing worse happens. What *did* happen last night?"

"We caught some bad men. Your boy friend's name was Elliott."

She sat motionless, elbow resting on the table and smoke curling up from her cigarette. When her face was in repose, as now, she had a classic beauty.

"So you found him."

"Elliott won't give us any more trouble."

"Is it—over?"

Ross said: "No, not quite."

"What do you mean by quite?"

"That we haven't caught them all," said Ross. "No reason why I shouldn't tell you that much, but I can't go too far, sweet. Against orders! I should say you can put a time limit to your fears."

"I wonder," said Mae.

Her bag was on a chair, nearby. She opened it and took out a folded newspaper, one of the *Daily Mirror* size, and all pictures and headlines. She unfolded it slowly, to the middle pages, and handed it to him. As he glanced down, he knew that she was watching him intently.

Alice Conway's photograph stared up at him; it took a quarter of the page. There was a news story with the headline: PROFESSOR'S DAUGHTER KIDNAPPED. He glanced up at her, and she didn't show any expression. He read the story, which told the simple truth, gave few details, and said that it was understood that security police were working against the kidnappers; and thus it went farther than it should have done, but would do no great harm.

"Is that the girl you want?" asked Mae.

"*What?*"

She smiled faintly.

"I mean, the girl you were asking me about—you wanted to know whether I'd seen one."

"Oh, that. Yes, that's the lady. Not bad to look at, is she?" asked Ross. "I think she's having a rough time. Recognise her?"

He forced the light note, was angry with himself because for a moment he had read the wrong meaning into her: "Is that the girl you want?" Mae couldn't guess the absurdity of his feelings, that haunting longing to find and know the girl whom he had seen for less than half an hour.

"Yes," said Mae.

His expression changed.

"What's this, Mae?"

"When you look like that I know what it must feel to be a man like Elliott with you after him," said Mae. "I've often seen her, Peter. She hasn't been there lately, but at one time she was often with Bray at the Dive and other places—before he took up with Dolly Leeming. I thought you ought to know."

CHAPTER 24
REUNION

It could be coincidence, but he didn't think it likely. He looked at Alice's picture and then at Mae, whose gravity was so unlike her that it was almost as if he were looking at a stranger. She finished her cigarette and stubbed it out in a saucer.

"Will it help?"

"It might, at that," said Ross. "I've never seen her at the Dive."

"No, she hasn't been there much lately," said Mae. "I haven't seen her for months, and I never knew her well. We'd say 'hallo', that was all. She seemed very young and too sweet to haunt the Dive with a man like Bray, but you can never tell with these innocents." Mae laughed, with a flash of her old self. "Have you seen Bray lately?"

He had to decide how much he should tell her.

"Yes."

"About this case?"

Ross smiled.

"I ought to call in Loftus, remember him?"

"I only want to know because I think I might be able to help," said Mae. "No, don't throw your hands up in horror, listen and be serious, darling. I *want* to help. Unless I do, I don't think I'll ever live down what I started the other night. Say I want to rehabilitate myself, and——"

"Damn it, you weren't as bad as that!"

"Peter, I'm *not* a fool," said Mae. "I can see that I was forcing you to think of me when you ought to have been concentrating on your job. For all I know, something went wrong because of it. Now I want to pull my weight. Just once—and I think there might be a way."

"Oh," said Ross, and didn't answer, just watched her with smiling eyes.

She lit another cigarette. Every movement she made had grace and beauty, she did the smallest things in a way which couldn't fail to attract attention; because she was what she was. Her beauty was near perfection, and yet it didn't give him what he had always believed possession of it would give.

"Let me see Bray," said Mae.

"But my sweet——"

"I know Bray," said Mae, almost contemptuously. "He seems a harmless little man, and probably he is. He'd do anything for money, and gives away a lot as a sop to his conscience. I think he's smart enough to fool you, darling. But I think I could get the truth out of him."

"I wonder."

"I know," said Mae, emphatically.

"What would you try to find out?"

Mae tapped the picture.

"You want to find Alice Conway, don't you? He may have some idea about her—after all, he was all for her until he met Dolly. Usually, he makes friends because of what he wants to get, and he wanted something from Alice Conway. It should be possible to find out what he was after and whether he got it."

"I see," said Ross.

The two motives were warring with each other again. He did not think that Mae could do anything useful; but if she were allowed to try, it might help her.

"Tell me I'm a fool," said Mae.

"But you've just said you're not!" He leaned forward and patted her hand. "I'll have a word with my boss."

Mae's eyes glowed.

Craigie was still looking tired when Ross arrived at the office, half an hour later. He was alone. As always, he dropped what he was doing, and seemed to be ready to give all his attention to Ross. Nothing hurried and nothing flurried him—and in a moment of detachment, Ross marvelled at the man's qualities.

He talked...

"Bill Loftus half-suggested that we might try to get her to help—as a solution to your emotional problem," said Craigie. "I didn't think it was the right one. Think she might do anything with Bray?"

"It's possible."

"Do you think Bray's still in the running?"

Ross shrugged.

"The evidence all suggests that he was framed, but he may be in deeper than he admits. Or he may have been in deeper once. That's one thing we've never checked—the reason why he allowed himself to be blackmailed. At least, I haven't."

"We've tried, but don't yet know the secret."

"It could be this. Supposing he was in the business at the start, and worked on Alice Conway—and supposing he got cold feet. That would give the others a pretty strong hold on him."

"Could be," agreed Craigie.

Ross said slowly: "Did you get anything from those offices last night? Anything that matters, or might show the way to Alice?"

"Not the second," said Craigie, and took his meerschaum from the desk and began to fill it from a flat tin of tobacco. "They've another hide-out, and although we alerted the police in London and the Home Counties, we didn't get any news about them. We don't know how many there were, except that there are indications that at least four people were working in that underground office. Most of the papers had been taken away—secret papers, that is. We found one empty filing-drawer, and a safe was open. There was a legitimate business—importing and exporting—which was obviously a cover for the real activities. They vanished—and left us with exactly the same problem, but with fewer men to look for."

"What about Elliott and Higson?"

"They haven't said a word—and I doubt if we can make them."

"Don't we have our methods?"

"It's nearly got past that stage, but I'll have a shot," said Craigie. "None of this has run according to normal form. It reminds me of a ship with watertight compartments—they keep getting through one section, and we come up against the next door. But there'll be an end to it. I still think the most important thing is to find Alice Conway."

Ross said slowly: "Yes. Gordon, I've got a notion which might be crazier than anything else."

"What?"

"Could the *Conways* be in this?"

Craigie didn't answer, didn't say no, didn't suggest that he ruled the suggestion out of court. After a while, he lit his pipe and remarked:

"We don't know who's in it, and we don't know all their motives."

"So you've thought of it. The immediate question is to find out what Bray wanted with Alice Conway, isn't it?"

Craigie nodded.

"Going to let Mae try?"

"I think so."

"That'll please her." Ross leaned back in his chair, so that it balanced precariously on the back legs. "It might be an idea to let him have his Dolly back first; he'd really be in a happy mood, then."

Sammy Bray did not go to his office that morning, but had several telephone conversations with his secretary, all of them apparently on normal business; each was taken down in shorthand and carefully reported to Craigie within a few seconds of the conversation finishing. When he left the telephone, Bray went into the large and lovely drawing-room, and stood with his hands in his pockets, looking moodily out of the window. Now and again, he sighed.

A car drew up, and he craned his neck to try to see who came out, but it was too close to the door, and he couldn't tell whether it was a man or a woman. He turned away and looked at the telephone, actually went across and picked up the receiver, then put it down again. He had not yet made any complaint to his friends in high places or given any statement to a newspaper.

There was a ring at the front-door bell.

Watson appeared from the kitchen.

"If that is the man Ross, bring him in straight away," said Bray. "I wish to talk to him."

"Very good, sir."

Watson was unimpressed by the weighty manner of the instructions. Bray, frowning, went to his chair and sat down, expected to hear voices but heard none, then fancied he heard light footsteps. He started to his feet.

The door burst open, and Dolly came rushing in, beaming, eyes glistening.

"Darling!" cried Bray.

"Precious!" gasped Dolly.

Bray hugged her, Dolly gasped and squeezed him; they were breathless when they stood back; still holding each other's hands. Dolly was half a head taller, and compared with Bray, almost slender. She wore a black suit and a mink collar, her make-up was good, she was brimming over with happiness.

"*Sammy,*" she breathed.

"This is *wonderful,* my treasure!"

"I thought they were never going to release me," said Dolly. "Do give me a cigarette, and could I have a teeny-weeny drink? I know it's early, but I'm so thirsty and excited, I could dance!"

She backed away, squeezed his hands before freeing them, and pirouetted round. The flared skirt whirled up above her knees—Dolly had not been selected as a chorus girl for nothing, and she couldn't act. She finished, and collapsed into his arms.

"Wonderful!" bubbled Bray. "Marvellous!"

He poured drinks with an unsteady hand, was much more nervous than he had been with Ross. They clinked glasses. He stood and stared at her as she sat back, legs crossed, skirt modestly pulled low over her knees. She was fresh-skinned, her hair was hennaed to hide the greyness, she had good eyes and long lashes—there was a hint of blowsiness about her, a touch of coarseness, but she was good enough to look at.

Bray finished his drink.

"What happened?" he asked.

She'd been coming to see him when a man had stopped her, showed her a special police card, and taken her away; she had been *flabbergasted.* He'd taken her to a police station and spent a lot of time questioning her, mostly about Sammy Bray, and there wasn't a thing she knew that they wanted. They'd asked questions at various times, and she'd always told them the truth as far as she could, and:

"Honey, every time I could I told them what a wonderful man you are, I said you were *smashing*. I just wouldn't hear a word against you, and I wouldn't let them say anything, either. You should have heard me giving them a piece of my mind, you should, really."

"I wish I had," said Bray fervently. "Precious, they didn't ill-treat you?"

"Oh, *no*," said Dolly, "they were quite nice, really, although rather stern—you remember that policeman we had here when you'd left your car without lights, rather like *that*, only they were all in plain clothes. I couldn't understand it, I kept wondering why you didn't send for me, it wasn't as if I was under arrest. I kept protesting and protesting, and they fobbed me off with a lot of silly answers, but I suppose it doesn't really matter now, here I *am*."

Bray sealed that with a kiss.

"The things they wanted to know! All about your friends, Mae Harrison, you know *Mae*, a man named Tiger—do you know, I had to sit down and write out a list of everyone you knew. And you know how *hopeless* I am on names, darling, I could tell them their Christian names, but *couldn't* remember the surnames. It was funny, really, they thought I was lying to them, and I got all worked up and angry, and as soon as they saw that, they calmed down. They weren't satisfied until they were sure I'd remembered *everyone*. They even included Sam at the Dive, and everyone else there, and the Dive itself—oh, and there's *one* name they were very interested in."

She waggled a finger at him, and smiled as if reprovingly. Bray went across and patted her cheek.

"What name, sweet?"

"You'll *never* guess—Alice *Conway,*" said Dolly. "I didn't want to tell them about you and Alice, but they sprang it on me this morning, just before I came away. When they forced me to talk—well, they didn't exactly *force,* they made it very difficult not to, though, I told them how she was always trying to make you give her presents, and she clung like a leech—I told them a thing or two about Alice, believe me. I told them *everything* that you've ever told me about her, but I can't understand why they were interested in that little gold-digger, can you?"

"I most certainly *cannot,*" breathed Bray.

He didn't look so happy for a few moments, but soon recovered.

He sat opposite her, beaming, close enough to stretch out and touch her, blissfully quiet—and then the front-door bell rang. He thought immediately of Ross, and for the first time since Dolly had returned, he frowned. He heard Watson go across and open the door, and heard a woman's voice. Then:

"I will find out if he is in, Miss," said Watson.

"Why, who can *that* be?" asked Dolly, and put her head on one side roguishly. "You haven't been making new friends while poor little Dolly's been locked up, have you, precious?"

"Don't you worry," said Bray. "I can't imagine who this is——"

"Miss Harrison, sir," said Watson, coming in and closing the door.

"Mae!' exclaimed Dolly.

"Miss *Harrison.*"

"Yes, sir, she——"

"That's right," said Mae.

She opened the door and thrust her way past Watson, who waited for instructions from Bray and received them with a wave of the hand. Mae smiled across at Dolly, while Bray backed to his chair, struck against it with the back of his legs, and sat down heavily.

Chapter 25
A Little More?

"Why, Mae!" exclaimed Dolly brightly, "it *is* nice to see you, how are you, darling?" She took Mae's hand and put cheek to cheek, then backed away. "You look lovely—doesn't she look lovely, Sammy? She always does, you don't know how I envy you your figure, Mae, you never seem to put on an inch."

"Hallo," said Mae. "I do hope I haven't come at a bad time."

"Oh, of course not, Sammy and I like a bit of company," said Dolly. "True I've been away for a day or two, but there's plenty of time, isn't there, Sammy?"

She gave a little giggling laugh.

"Eh? Time—oh, yes. Plenty of time, all the time in the world," said Bray. "That is—Miss Harrison, I don't often have the pleasure of welcoming you here."

Mae said abruptly: "I want your help."

Bray looked puzzled, Dolly frowned and backed towards the cocktail cabinet, taking refuge in the thought of drinks. Mae took off her hat and brushed her fingers through her hair, and looked harassed and worried. She had on little make-up, there was a touch of eye-pencil just beneath her eyes, which made her seem tired.

"Gladly, gladly. But you'll have a drink, difficulties often dissolve over a drink!"

He chuckled heartily.

"May I have a gin and It?"

"Will you fix it, honey?" asked Bray. "My dear Miss Harrison, please sit down, I can tell you're worried. But it's probably nothing serious, you know, I've often been *very* worried without any cause at all—not any good cause."

"Oh, this is serious," said Mae, and laughed on a low note. "You know there's some trouble, don't you, about a missing Professor's daughter? A Professor Conway."

Bray shot Dolly a startled glance; Mae appeared not to notice it, and went on:

"The police think *I* know something about it."

Dolly gave a little squeaking sound, and Bray shook his head, as if this couldn't be true. Mae leaned back in her chair and closed her eyes. There was silence until Dolly came across with the glass in her hand.

"This'll do you good, Mae."

"Thanks so much." Mae sipped. "It's no secret, but Peter—you know Peter Ross, don't you—is a special kind of policeman. He's made it pretty obvious that I'm suspected, and so have others. I can't imagine why, except that I knew this girl slightly. It was only a nodding acquaintance, at the Dive." She glanced at Dolly. "Forgive me, Dolly, but— Mr. Bray knew her rather well."

Bray said: "Yes, yes."

"Don't worry about me," said Dolly quickly. "Sam doesn't keep any secrets from me, the past is the past, that's what we both believe in. Not that she was ever anything to him, the money-grubbing little——"

She broke off.

"What did she want?" asked Mae.

"Everything she could get."

Dolly was shrill.

Bray looked unhappy, and passed his hand over his forehead.

"I'm most distressed that you are in difficulties, Miss Harrison, I know what it is to be suspected of something you know nothing about. I only wish I could help you. As Dolly says, Alice Conway *was* rather pressing in her attentions, and—Dolly will understand—she is rather a sweet little woman——"

Dolly snorted.

"At all events, that was how she appeared to be," said Bray, firmly. "She had led a rather quiet life and didn't feel happy in the different surroundings at first, but she quickly became used to them. She came to me first for work, she said that she was tired of domestic work at home—her father is a widower, all the home responsibility fell on to Alice—and I could understand that. Unhappily, she had no qualifications, but I was rather—rather dazzled, I suppose." He looked at Dolly almost challengingly, and she pouted but made no comment. "Mind you, she was an intelligent young woman, with training she would do very well, I imagine, but I couldn't employ an untrained girl in my rather complicated business. I befriended her, and—then I met Dolly."

"I see," said Mae, and leaned back, looking tired and weary. "There's nothing else?"

"I'm afraid not—I only wish I could help you in some way."

"How did you break the friendship?"

Bray coloured.

"It was rather embarrassing. I fear that I must have given her the wrong idea, and—but does it matter? She was offended, perhaps hurt, but I had to be firm. It is distressing, talking about things like this, but I can understand your distress, and Dolly——"

"Don't worry about me." Dolly went across and sat on the arm of his chair, putting a hand at his neck and toying with the short, fluffy hairs. "What on earth makes them suspect *you*, Mae? I know Sammy wouldn't turn on me if *I* was in any kind of trouble."

"Dolly!" Bray protested.

Dolly pursed her lips, as if to say: "Facts are facts and you can't alter them."

"Did Alice Conway have any close friends?" asked Mae.

"I really don't know. She didn't introduce any to me, in fact she talked very little about her private life. Very little indeed, except—that she was unhappy at home. I gathered that her father was very preoccupied, paid her little attention, and that life was very dull."

"I see," said Mae. "You've been very good." She picked up her gloves and bag and stood up. Bray rose and shook hands, and Dolly darted towards the door.

"I'll see Mae out, honey, you sit back."

"Well—very well. Good-bye, Miss Harrison. Every good wish."

He watched the two women go out; probably he noticed that Dolly closed the door. He could not have heard her whisper, with a hand tight on Mae's arm.

"He's so soft-hearted, any little brat can make a fool of him. All she wanted was his money, she thought she was on a good thing. It's a good thing for Sammy that I came along, she would have fleeced him. Don't make any mistake about *that*."

"No," said Mae. "I won't."

Ross stood as Mae told the story. She remembered it in detail, could quote Bray time and time again. She didn't seem to suspect that she was drawing a picture which made mockery of Ross's opinion of a pair of blue eyes. He stood rock-like in front of the empty fireplace, interjecting a question now and again, so as to get the picture much more clearly.

"I hope it's helped," Mae finished.

"Oh, it's helped," said Ross. "We've a clearer picture of Alice Conway, and we know she was after our Sammy. And I don't have to tell you what that seems to mean."

"She wanted money, and didn't much mind how she got it," said Mae.

Ross nodded.

Craigie and Loftus were in the office when Ross reached there, immediately after the talk with Mae. Loftus made shorthand notes as the story was repeated, and needed to ask no questions. Craigie was doodling with a pencil, drawing Red Indians in full battle-dress.

Ross finished, and waited.

"So Alice was after the money-bags, if we can believe all this," Loftus mused.

"That's what the indications say." Ross lit a cigarette from the stub of another. "And if she'd try to get it that way, she mightn't care how she got her hands on it. I took her word for it that she'd been kidnapped and knew nothing about the business, but it's possible that she was playing with fire, and got burnt. Also possible——" He broke off.

"Let's have it," said Loftus.

"Well, you may as well," said Ross. "It's also possible that she's working with these people, that she was tied up to make it look as if she were a victim, and pulled the wool nicely over my eyes."

"Could be."

Craigie glanced up from his doodling.

"Then why is she still captive?" asked Loftus.

Ross shrugged.

"Oh, tell me I'm guessing and out of my depth. I'll be with you all the way."

"Haven't you missed something?" Craigie asked mildly. "Or don't you want us to see what's in your mind?"

Ross said: "I don't want to show any prejudice for Blue-eyed Alice Conway, but I could ask myself why she was really getting at Bray. Did she know that her father was in danger, had she any reason to think that Bray was behind it? That could be, too."

"Like me to see Conway, or will you?" asked Loftus.

The Professor's house was an old-fashioned one in a terrace, and Ross reached it a little before two o'clock. One of Craigie's men was sitting at the wheel of a small car, farther along the street, and Ross walked past him. The agent winked; which meant that all seemed well at the Conway *ménage*. Ross hadn't really seen Conway as his normal self, but remembered the way in which the man had leaned back in the arm-chair; and how he had looked dead. He had not left the house since his return from the nursing-home. No one except Craigie's men had followed him.

A middle-aged woman opened the door; Conway had a sister who had come to look after him while he was recovering from the morphia. She was fussy and a little agitated, made him wait in the hall, and came from a room on the right after several minutes, straightening a wisp of grey hair.

"The Professor *can* see you, Mr. Ross, but please don't stay too long and don't make him talk too much, he isn't *well*. He's been working too hard for years, I've always told him so, and now he has the worry about his daughter. It's a wicked shame, that's the only word for it."

"Yes," said Ross, and smiled.

He won an answering smile as Conway's sister opened the door.

Conway sat in an arm-chair in a book-lined room. Untidiness was the keynote. A large pedestal desk was littered with papers, papers and pamphlets were on top of the books in the bookshelves, oddments dotted the floor, several books were open on the floor near the Professor's chair. It was an unlikely repository for vital defence secrets. Conway started to rise.

"Hallo, sir," said Ross. "No, don't get up."

"You're very kind. Please sit down."

Ross moved yet another book from a comfortable, old-fashioned chair on the other side of the fireplace, and made himself at ease.

"Mind if I smoke?"

"By no means. Mr. Ross, have you any news of my daughter?"

Ross said: "I'm afraid not."

There was little change in Conway's expression, and he always looked a sick man. He was paler than when Ross had seen him before, and seemed to have become thinner. There were scraggy bags of flesh under his chin—he wore a winged collar—and his eyes were heavy and glassy, as if he hadn't slept for days. He was old; there were browny-blue freckles on the backs of his hands, and the skin had a kind of transparency, the veins showed up very blue. Ross felt a sense of shock; that so much depended on a man as old as this, and in such a condition. Conway was one of many, but everyone acknowledged his supremacy in his own branch of the atomic field.

He didn't speak.

"But we've caught several of the people concerned, I don't think it'll be long before it's over," said Ross. "You haven't had a message?"

"Nothing—nothing at all. If I had, I would have reported it immediately, Mr. Ross. I have Mr. Loftus's number. He has been very good, everyone has been most kind, but—I feel as if only part of me is here. I've had time to think, too, I've taken Alice too much for granted. She's been here most of the time, sacrificed much of her life for me, her opportunities, perhaps her hopes. She seemed so willing, but now that she may not come back——" He closed his eyes.

"I shouldn't assume that yet."

"It is difficult to be optimistic," said Conway. "I don't quite know why, I feel as if she's gone never to return. And I've been wondering how much I robbed her of, Mr. Ross. That's not a consoling thought."

"Probably of nothing," Ross said.

The Professor's conscience was pricking him, and this squared with what Bray had told Mae. Ross looked into the faded blue eyes, and eyes of brighter blue seemed to be superimposed upon them. Was he completely inane in thinking that she had meant everything she had said at Shepperton?

"Professor, did she change her habits at all, a few months ago?"

"Change? No. Not in any way."

"Was she out more, in the evenings?"

"Well—yes, perhaps she was, but I wouldn't call that a *change*. She studied drawing at an art school some nights, made friends with a girl who lived very close to the school, and—but I hardly see the point of this question, Mr. Ross."

"It's just background. Did you know a man named Bray—Samuel Bray?"

"No," said the Professor, promptly.

"Did you ever hear your daughter mention the name?"

"I really don't remember it," said the Professor, "although she often talked about people at the art school and friends she made, I'm afraid I didn't pay much attention. I've been obsessed with my work—too obsessed, no doubt. How will this—ah—background help you to find Alice?"

He was pathetic.

Ross said: "Among her acquaintances we might find the man who took her off. She'd be more likely to go with someone she knew than with a stranger. What's your own theory of the motive, Professor?"

"Do you need telling?" Conway smiled faintly, not with amusement. "These misguided people think that they can bring pressure to bear upon me. You think so, too, or you wouldn't have had me followed, wouldn't have my house watched and wouldn't ask me if I'd heard from Alice. There are great tensions in loyalties, Mr. Ross, but I don't think you need fear. Alice would be the first to agree that sacrifices sometimes have to be made for great causes, and surely one's own country is a great cause. Alice would think so—patriotism was almost a passion with her."

The Professor pressed his hands against his forehead.

Ross stood up, and felt like a clod.

"I won't worry you any more, sir. We'll do everything we can to find her."

"I know you will," said Conway.

Ross went to shake hands and caught sight of a photograph on the mantelpiece, turned so that Conway could see it easily but hiding the face from anyone who sat in the chair opposite. It was the original of the picture which the newspaper had used—and it was coloured. The blueness of Alice's eyes was so deep and clear that it looked unnatural, as if the artist had striven to improve on nature. In fact, those eyes were exactly as Ross remembered them.

She had lied to Conway about the art school, had spent those nights at the Dive—partly with Bray. With anyone else, too?

Why had she chosen Bray? Had chance thrown them together, or was Bray lying? Had he sought her out, or had she made a dead set at him?

Bray seemed so transparently honest now.

Conway's sister opened the door, and the telephone bell rang. Ross hesitated, heard Conway answer, and then a call:

"Rosie—Rosie, is Mr. Ross still here?"

"Why, yes!"

"There's a telephone call for him," said Conway.

Chapter 26
Crack

"Peter?"

It was Loftus.

"Yes."

"Get here at once," Loftus said. "Elliott's cracked, I think we're nearly home. Anything your end?"

"No."

"I shouldn't think the Professor's in it himself," said Loftus, "but a woman is highly placed. Elliott got most of his orders from her."

"Well, well," said Ross.

The Professor was looking at a newspaper, and paid no attention to Ross, who put down the receiver, thanked the old man, and was shown out fussily by the woman. He nodded to the Department Z man as he sped past, and reached Whitehall in record time.

Williamson was in the office with the two regulars, leaning back and smoking, looking lazy and contented. Craigie was smiling, Loftus had lost much of the tension which he'd shown for days. Ross felt no easing in the tension, and asked himself what they would think if they knew the drift of his talk. He ought to have withdrawn, ought not to have allowed Craigie to talk him into staying on the job. He'd gone emotionally soft, and knew it.

He didn't show it.

"Now what's all this?"

"Tim spent a couple of hours with Elliott," Loftus said cheerfully, "and Elliott couldn't stand the strain. We know most of the game, now. It's purely private enterprise—these people have been selling information to the biggest buyer for a long time. A small but effective international spy-ring, with wares more or less on the open market. Elliott, Higson, and two or three others have been in it together, and there are unknowns—just telephone voices, to Elliott. One was a woman. He had two telephone numbers to contact her, and we've checked them both. One is at Watford, and I've a party on the way out there. The other, which Elliott used more often, in Wimbledon—a big house, not far from the Common. He spoke to her at that number some hours before you caught him, last night. She told him he could meet Bray, and also told him to take that wig and false nose along. She's given detailed instructions all along the line, there isn't much doubt that she runs the show."

"Well, well!" exclaimed Ross.

"The place is already surrounded, but we're letting anyone who arrives go in, and allowing anyone to leave—we'll pick them up some distance from the house. We'll raid it after dark, and that gives you about four hours' sleep."

"Who wants sleep?" asked Ross.

"You do. Tim does. Everyone who's going into that raid needs to be fresh, and after last night you're not so fresh as you should be."

Ross frowned.

"I'm not so sure. Did Elliott say why they made a set at getting me off the job?"

"Because it was known you were watching Conway," said Craigie. "Don't ask us how they knew, Peter, and take Bill's advice. When the job's over, you can ask all the questions you want to."

"I'll be good," said Ross.

As he drove back to his flat, he couldn't make out his own reactions. It was a kind of exhilaration, because the end was surely in sight, merged with edginess, because he was afraid of what he was going to learn. Craigie was right; Craigie was pretty well always right; he needed rest and could worry later about reasons for what had happened. This case was a perfect example of how the Department worked, and how little really depended on one individual. He'd tried Conway and missed; Williamson, who had a knack of breaking down a prisoner's resistance, had pulled his job off. Craigie and Loftus chose the men for special jobs unerringly—the only mistake they had made was with him!

He left the car in a nearby garage, and walked towards his flat. He was extra careful, until he saw one of the Department's younger agents; Craigie wasn't taking any chances. The man winked, the all-clear signal. Yet Ross was cautious as he went in, and glanced into all the rooms before he felt completely at ease. He locked and bolted both the back and front doors, and went to his bedroom. He was used to sleeping at odd hours, and now that he knew he had a chance to relax, he wanted sleep. Trust Craigie to be right! He laughed to himself as he took off his shoes, collar and tie, then his coat, and lay down with an eiderdown over him. He stared at the ceiling for a while, then began to see pictures—of Alice Conway looking at him out of a newspaper and from the mantelpiece at Conway's house.

It was nearly half past four.

He turned over, and willed sleep…

The ringing of the telephone bell woke him, and he blinked in the fading light. The bell next to his bed kept ringing, and he turned over and took off the receiver. All that Craigie had said flooded into his mind; thought of the coming raid; thought of Alice Conway.

"Hallo?"

"Wakie-wakie," Loftus said, cheerfully.

"Oaf!"

"You're due at Crossways, Wimbledon Common, at nine o'clock, and it's now just turned eight," said Loftus.

"That's easy. Anything else?"

"Two men have gone into the house, no one has come out. There's a garbled story from a neighbouring gardener that a woman was carried in there on a stretcher the other day, but I wouldn't like to rely on it too much, he waffles. The house has been rented furnished for the past four months, and Higson of the Dive signed the lease."

"We certainly aren't a thousand miles away," Ross said. "What are you keeping me talking for?"

Loftus laughed, and rang off.

Ross put on his shoes, and had one tied when the telephone bell rang again. Mae? He hesitated; it might be wise not to talk to anyone, he hadn't a lot of time. Nonsense? He lifted the receiver.

A man said: "You've had plenty of warnings, Ross."

It wasn't *the* voice; obviously it couldn't be Elliott's. The old trick was being tried by someone else. Ross caught his breath, and the man at the other end of the line chuckled.

"You'll regret being obstinate," he said. "You'll regret it a lot."

He rang off.

Ross stared down at the untied lace of his right shoe, and did nothing about it. The new warning had shocked him more than anything in the affair; it was completely unexpected; these devils were still sure of themselves. Slowly, he knotted the lace, and straightened up. He put on his collar and tie, and watched his expression in the mirror; it reflected the shock and the grimness that was in him.

He filled his two automatic pistols, slipped one into his hip pocket and another into his shoulder holster. He fastened a thin, sheathed knife inside his waist-band. The Department sometimes used other weapons, but Loftus would be on the job tonight, and would have everything required for the raid. Tear-gas, probably. He was going to the door when he swung round, hurried to the telephone, and dialled Craigie's number.

"Loftus," said Loftus.

"Peter Ross—SSOR. Bill, I've just had another 'keep out' warning."

"Well, well," breathed Loftus. "We aren't quite through yet. How long ago?"

"Five minutes."

'Then it wasn't Bray, or we'd have had word that he'd called you," said Loftus. "From Crossways, possibly. All set to go?"

"Fully loaded."

Loftus chuckled; he was always in a brighter mood when he thought the end of a chase was near. He knew that there might be casualties in the raid, possibly heavy casualties, yet he was cheerful.

"Don't break your neck on the way."

"No, sir," said Ross with mock humility.

He banged down the receiver, and went towards the little hall—and caught sight of the newspaper with Alice

Conway's photograph in; he had left it on a chair, folded with her picture uppermost. He glowered at it, and stepped to the door—and the door bell rang.

"Now listen," he said *sotto voce*. "I'm in a hurry."

He moved into the front room, pulled aside the curtain, and saw the Department's watchdog on duty; so the caller was someone who seemed reliable and safe. But he didn't want to talk to anyone, he hadn't much time. It was already much darker than when he had woken up—and the light was on. Whoever was outside knew that he was in. He could slip out the back way, but—why? A few minutes wouldn't make all that difference, they would wait for him at Wimbledon. He went back to the hall, and in spite of the reassurance of the man outside, he stood to one side as he opened the door, so that he couldn't be shot at as it opened.

Mae stood there.

"Hallo!" greeted Ross, after a brief pause. "We don't have the luck, sweet, I'm just off out."

"We have some luck," Mae said. "You're still alive." She stepped in, and closed the door behind her, and took his hand. "Darling, I just have to talk to you."

"Mae——"

"I must!"

She held his hand, and he could feel the pressure of her fingers and the quivering of her nerves. She was pale; he thought 'distraught'. He couldn't understand it, unless she thought that she had news. Minutes wouldn't matter, but he mustn't stay longer. If he refused to listen, she would feel as if he'd struck her.

He freed his arm and squeezed her waist.

"Can it be quick, darling?"

"I'll be as quick as I can," said Mae.

She was breathing heavily as she led the way into the living-room. It was only a few days ago that she had come in here unexpectedly, using her own key, and his heart leapt and started to race as if he had never seen a beautiful woman before; she had been everything that was desirable. Was it her fault that he didn't think that now, or had the change been in him?

He knew the answer. He frowned.

Mae didn't seem to notice that.

"Didn't you get your key back?" he asked.

"Oh, yes, I forgot it," said Mae.

She took off her hat and tossed it to a chair, almost indecent treatment for a model that had cost a small fortune. She pushed her fingers through her hair in the way she had, and now he could see that her eyes were glittering, as if she had a severe headache; or was feverish. He'd never seen her look like this before.

"Well, my sweet?"

The hands of the clock on the mantelpiece pointed to eight-twenty-five, and he would be late. He ought to have gone out the back way.

"Peter—where are you going?"

"Oh, come," he said. "You don't have to be told that I've some odds and ends to do."

"On this—case?"

He didn't answer.

"You're—not—to—go," said Mae.

Each word came slowly and distinctly. She backed a pace, as if she wanted to get between him and the door. She meant everything she said, she hadn't been able to stand the strain. It hurt; and it told him that whatever happened in the future, for him it would not hold Mae. The last lingering doubt went then. She'd told him she couldn't stand the strain, and she was right; just as he had been right with Craigie. But he had to stand it.

"Listen, my darling," he said softly. "I've a job to do, and I must do it. We'll talk afterwards."

"You're not to go," Mae said more quickly. "I've just had—a message."

"Oh?"

"From a man who said——"

She caught her breath, went forward, and gripped his hands and pressed them against her breast. She kissed him suddenly and fiercely, and he could feel her warm breath mingling with his. He nearly lost his balance, steadied, and took her wrists.

"What man, and what did he say?"

"I don't know the man. He said that you wouldn't get back alive if you went to work tonight."

"Nonsense. Cheap threats——"

"It wasn't a cheap threat, he meant what he said. Don't you understand, you'll be walking into a trap, they know you're going, and you'll have no chance. Peter, I can't let you go, I *won't* let you go."

"Stay here until I get back," he said more gently.

"No!" she cried. She flung herself at him again and imprisoned his arms, and she had more strength than he realised. "I can't let you, you'll be walking to your death, there's no need for it. Peter, don't you understand? I love you, I'd do anything to save you, you mustn't die. You don't owe this work your life, you owe that to me. You mustn't go!"

"We'll talk later," he said, and had to exert a lot of pressure to move her away from him. She clutched at his coat, and pulled it open as he backed away. "Mae, I'm sorry, but I'm late already."

"Sorry!" she cried.

She snatched at the gun in his shoulder holster, drew it out and backed away. Her eyes were blazing, her lips twisted back from her teeth.

"I won't let you go! Don't move."

Chapter 27
Struggle

Ross didn't try to get the gun back. Mae whisked away from him, and it was out of reach. She pointed it at his chest, and her hand was unsteady, he believed that in her frenzy she would do anything to stop him. He didn't move his hand towards the other gun, she might realise what he was doing. He'd turned full circle, and she was fighting desperately against the thing she said she had accepted as inevitable.

He felt compassion for her. Slowly, the compassion faded.

"Peter, I'm serious," she said, and backed farther away. "I'll wound you so that you can't leave, if you try to go. I'm not going to let them kill you."

"They've often tried, Mae."

"This time they'll succeed."

"You're not yourself," he said. "Listen, my pet. We've talked this out several times, and we'll have another session later. Just now I've a job to do that must be done, and if you stopped me, you'd never forgive yourself. And—*I'd* never forgive you."

"You'd live to be grateful."

"Not for this. Mae, if you want to hold my respect, put that gun down and see this my way."

"Respect!"

"You need it for a basis for marriage."

"I can't marry a corpse."

He held her gaze for what seemed a long time, and the gun kept pointing at his chest. Then he moved—not backwards, but sideways and forward, leaping at her. She fired. The bullet tore through his coat and thudded into the door, but it didn't hurt him. He reached her and thrust the gun aside, but she didn't lose her grip on it. He clutched at her wrist, and she twisted and turned furiously, she was like quicksilver. He would never have believed that she had such strength. He got a grip at last, and twisted.

She gave a stifled scream, and dropped the gun. He kicked it across the carpet. The sound of the shot would have reached the man outside, he would be rushing towards the flat by now. In a few seconds it would be over, but it had lasted long enough to force a physical struggle— to make the impossible real. Mae stood holding her wrist, glaring at him; there was no other word for it, she didn't look sane. The only colour was lipstick and rouge, and the rouge seemed to burn, there were two spots of angry red on her cheeks. Her lips were still drawn back, she had a feline beauty—the kind of beauty he'd never really seen, although she'd hinted at it. This capacity for passion was the thing which had first attracted him, and it was too strong, he could never live with it.

There was a thunderous knocking at the front door.

"I'm sorry, Mae," he said.

He backed towards the gun, and shouted: "All safe!" for the benefit of the man outside. He picked the gun up, without once taking his gaze off Mae. Then he backed out of the room, closing the door a little with his foot. He backed to the front door and opened it.

"What the devil——" began the younger man outside.

"Just make sure she doesn't get away," Ross said. "She isn't quite herself. She——"

He saw astonishment on the face of Craigie's agent—and then the man pushed him aside violently. He staggered against the wall, as a shot rang out—a sharp crack, not the roar of a large automatic or a revolver. He saw the hole leap into the other's forehead, while he was still staggering. He caught a glimpse of Mae, with a tiny gun in her hand, turning towards him. He brought his own gun up, and fired; the shots were simultaneous, the roar of his drowned hers. He felt the knife-like pain of a bullet in his left arm—and saw her gun fly from her grip. Blood leapt on to her pale, slender hand; he'd hit it on the fingers and below the wrist. She stood quite still, glaring.

He said heavily: "You're not sane."

She didn't answer.

He glanced at the other agent, and knew that Craigie would soon have to make another entry in his black book. He had really turned full circle, now—love to hate. He felt a sudden, wild desire to laugh. Love to hate!

He motioned to her with the gun.

"Turn round, Mae."

She didn't move.

"Turn round," he said wearily, "and walk into the bedroom. I'm not going to hurt you, but I have to telephone for someone to come here. You'll be all right, don't worry."

She didn't move.

"Mae, don't be silly. I don't *want* to hurt you."

He hardly knew what he was saying.

"Well," she said in a slow voice, as if articulation were difficult and hurtful, "you have. I've tried to save you, but you haven't a chance. I've done everything *I* could, although you've just ignored me. I couldn't help falling in love with you, and if you'd been sensible, this—needn't have happened."

He stood rigid.

The truth came as a flash of lightning, vivid enough to blind him, but after that frightening moment he knew that it had been there from the beginning for him to see. *Mae* had wanted to stop him from working; *Mae* had clutched at him as Dolly clutched at Sammy Bray. Mae was working on the other side.

"It's your own fault," she choked. "I knew you were working on the Conway job, *mine* was to stop you. I'd got to know you so that I could spy on you, and—I fell in love with you. I fought for you, if it hadn't been for me, you would have been killed long ago. Until you got to the Dive, no one tried to kill you. I wouldn't allow it. I thought——"

She broke off.

"All right, Mae," said Ross. "Get out of the way. I've a job to finish."

He might have to kill her; at least to wound her again.

"You and your work, that's all you think about, you'd sacrifice everything for it. You were ready to sacrifice me when you didn't know—the truth. Well, you're not going to finish that job."

His mind was beginning to work more freely. She had told him about the garage and Tiger's house—*after* Tiger was dead. She had made a complete fool of him from the beginning, and he hadn't once dreamed of it. He'd even let her 'help'—and Craigie and Loftus had fallen for that one.

"What do you think you'll get out of it?" he asked.

"I'll get Conway," she said. "It's taken until now to break down his daughter's resistance, but now she's going to beg him to help. He'll rush to help her and walk into the trap, we'll get him again. We've always meant to get him."

"Who? Why?"

Loftus had been so sure that these were independent spies; which meant she was doing this for money.

Time was ticking away; Loftus would not wait indefinitely. Who and why didn't matter, he could find all that out later. He felt weary enough to drop. She stood against the front door, hands stretched out to prevent him from getting at it, and he would have to shoot her or fight again. Blood dripped from her hand.

She drew in a shivering breath.

"Peter, why don't you see when you're beaten? Give it up. You and I together can——"

"We can't do anything together," he said. "I'll give you one minute to come away from that door."

She stiffened, and then came slowly towards him. She wasn't giving up, was still trying to win. Her hands stretched out, and she seemed oblivious of the pain in her hand. Each drip of blood seemed to hurt him. She was only two yards away, and moved slowly and steadily. Her eyes were glowing, as with fire.

"Peter, we—can—still——"

The door behind her burst open, a man appeared, gun in hand, and lost a precious second in his surprise at seeing them standing together. Ross didn't recognise him, and fired. He struck the man's gun arm and the gun went flying. The shot roared out through the open door, this one must have been heard outside. Ross leapt towards the man who was staggering back. Mae clutched at him, and he flung her off, reached the man and struck him savagely on the temple; he went down like a stone.

Mae grabbed at his arm.

"Peter, don't go, don't go!" She sobbed the words. "Don't leave me, don't go."

He couldn't go and leave her like she was, she was well enough to get away, there was no telling what devilry she might do then. She would be better dead. He felt a sudden, all-devouring desire to kill her. He flung her away, and she knocked against a chair, arms still spread out, eyes glowing with that unholy fire. He could shoot her, and no one would know that he could have avoided it.

"Peter," she moaned.

He heard running footsteps; he hadn't much time. His gun pointed towards her breast. With a slight squeeze of the trigger, she would die; there would be no clearing up to do, no trial, no turning of the sword in the wound of his folly.

Two men were rushing up the steps.

"Peter." He could hardly hear her voice. "Don't let them—catch me."

So she wanted to die.

Slowly, with a physical effort, he lowered the gun. Two men rushed in, one a policeman, the other in ordinary clothes. They drew up for a moment when they saw the man on the floor, and Mae. Ross glanced towards them—and Mae darted forward towards the second man's gun, which was on the floor a few inches from his hand. Ross grabbed at her and missed, she snatched the gun up and turned it towards herself. Ross leapt and struck her arm aside. The bullet smacked into the floor, the report was deafening.

Mae stood swaying, glaring.

The policeman, like a herald of doom, took her left arm firmly.

"Don't let's have any more of *this*," he said.

Mae looked at him—and began to laugh. She flung back her head and opened her mouth wide, and the laughter pealed out; it wasn't sane. *She* wasn't sane. Ross forced himself to look away from her, and caught the bewildered eye of the man who had come in with the policeman. He was not remarkable, just a well-dressed, youngish man.

"Are you in this?" Ross asked.

"*I'm* not in anything, I just happened to be passing."

"Oh. Help the policeman, will you, I've a job to do."

"You can't do anything now, you need a doctor." The stranger looked at Ross's left hand. Blood had trickled from the wound in his arm and was spreading over the back of his hand; he hadn't noticed it. He laughed shortly, swung round, snatched a linen towel off the bathroom rail, and wound it round his hand loosely. "Now we won't spoil the carpet," he said.

He tossed his Special Branch card to the policeman and went towards the door. Mae was still laughing, but not so loudly; she looked ill. He turned from the door and sent one look at her, and wondered what had happened to her beauty and what had warped her mind.

Then he went out.

It was ten minutes to nine.

The drive had made his wounded arm much more painful, towards the end of the run he found difficulty in using it for the wheel or the gears. He swung round a corner too fast, and saw a car pulled up across the road and two uniformed policemen standing in front of it. He jammed on his brakes. As he switched off the engine he heard a sound which was becoming familiar—the roar of a shot. There were two more, in quick succession, before one of the policemen came up.

Ross got out of the car, and bent his arm across his chest. "Having fun?" he asked.

The policeman's face was hardly visible in the dim light of a street lamp.

"I'm sorry, sir, you can't pass here, we're having some trouble. The best way——"

"It's my trouble," Ross said. "I'm expected. My name's Ross."

"Oh, yes, sir! Mr. Loftus said he was expecting you. Take the next turning, and be careful, they're firing at anything they can see. That's the house," he added, and pointed.

Ross could just see a house against the sky, some distance from this spot.

"Thanks," he said.

When he turned the corner, he saw two cars drawn up outside the gates of the house, more policemen and a man in plain clothes; so they'd had to call in the police. As he approached the gate, a shot rang out; he didn't know whether it was intended for him. He turned into the gateway, and saw Loftus and two or three other agents standing in a clump of bushes; Loftus was crouching. There was no light in the house, until a flash lit up a window for a moment— and there was an answering shot from the garden.

Ross reached Loftus.

"You've taken your time," said Loftus. "You can talk. I thought you'd run into a wall."

"Not the usual kind of wall," said Ross. "What's the situation?"

"I don't know how many of them are inside, but they're making it as hot as they can. Not much doubt that Alice Conway's with them, they say they'll kill her if we don't let them go. The usual desperate tactics. What happened to you?"

"I was just dealing with the leader of this mob," said Ross.

Loftus said: *"What?"*

Two others—Williamson and Perry—were within earshot, and they drew nearer. Another burst of shooting came from a different part of the grounds; Loftus undoubtedly had groups of men here, and there would also be strong forces of police.

"Serious?" asked Williamson.

"Full story later, but it was Mae," said Ross. "We can see the wood for the trees now, can't we? So Alice Conway's in there, and they'll kill her if we don't give them a free passage. Didn't Craigie say he wanted her, dead or alive, and it didn't much matter which?"

"This is the last stage," said Loftus. "We're getting closer, and their ammunition will give out. We'll start a rush soon, and use tear-gas, she'll have a fifty-fifty chance."

"Tried talking to them?"

"It's a waste of time," said Loftus.

"Talking usually is. Well, first I had to get Conway dead or alive, and next his daughter. Why don't I do something about it?"

Ross laughed, and that reminded him of Mae. He could see the way the others looked at him and guessed what they were thinking. They were thinking that he must have had a demoralising shock, and that he hated the world—because they thought the woman he loved had proved to be bad. They didn't know that he was sizzling with rage at his own folly.

"Peter, you drop back," said Loftus. "You're hurt, aren't you?"

"Just a scratch," said Ross. "When I'm inside the house, you can lead the light brigade, old chap."

He swung round, reached the drive, and raced towards the house.

CHAPTER 28
ALICE

As he ran, the shooting started. A piercing whistle came from behind him, a signal of some kind. He heard a bullet strike the drive in front of him, thought that another pulled at his coat, but he ran on, gun in hand. A fusillade of shots rang out from behind him. He had the wit to realise that Loftus had ordered general fire, at the blast of the whistle. The house seemed a long way off, but he went swiftly. He felt something snatch at his wounded arm, and there was more pain, but it hardly made him flinch.

The house was much nearer.

He swerved to one side, where he saw a window; he hadn't seen any shooting coming from that window, but there was plenty from another, near it. He reached the window, and smashed his gun against the glass. It broke with an explosive crack which sounded high above the shooting.

He knew he was crazy; and also knew that he had to do this thing; it was a form of penance—payment for folly. He smashed at the big splinters of glass which stuck out from the frame, then lowered his head and climbed through. Glass pulled at the towel and it unwound. He stepped inside the room and made for the door. Luck was with him, nothing was in his way. He was near the door when it burst open, and against a poor light, he saw a man rushing in. He fired; the man went down.

He thought he heard someone else at the window. The shooting was still going on, from inside and outside. He went into the passage, and there was no one in sight. The light was on the landing, just a dim glow. The stairs were wide and carpeted. He raced up them, pain forgotten. The noise of shooting seemed louder, now. As he reached the landing, where several doors were open, a man appeared, gun in hand. Ross shot him.

He went into the room and snatched at the light switch; the window was open, a breeze blew the curtains, but no one was there. Now, men were running up the stairs, Loftus had sent the others after him. He swung out of this room into another, from which the shooting sounded loud. As he pressed down the switch, he saw a man kneeling by the open window—and he saw Alice Conway lying on a bed; he didn't know whether she was dead or alive. The man at the window swung round, but was dazzled by the light. Ross shot the gun out of his hand.

Williamson came to the door.

"Careful," said Ross. "My job's over."

He went across to the bed. Alice was tied to it, hand and foot, her arms stretched above her head, she couldn't move. But her eyes were wide open, and the light shone on to their eternal blueness, which danger and fear could not take away. He didn't know whether she recognised him, but he stood looking down at her, smiling.

"It's all over," he said. "You're safe, and your father is safe. Nothing to worry about." He felt a wave of dizziness, staggered, recovered, and put his hand to his hip pocket and drew out a knife. "I'm quite good at doing this kind of thing," he said, and began to cut the cords.

He swayed again. The knife glinted and became a monstrous shining thing, then became absurdly small. He gritted his teeth, became steadier, and with great deliberation, cut all the cords. Then he dropped the knife.

"Take it easy," Williamson said.

He came farther into the room. Ross turned towards him, and realised vaguely that the shooting had stopped. Then he saw Loftus limping in, and Loftus was smiling. He let Williamson lead him across to a chair, leaned back, and closed his eyes. He heard Williamson speak as if from a long distance.

"He's lost a hell of a lot of blood."

As if that mattered.

Ross lay in bed in a room at a nursing-home near his flat, and looked idly through the newspapers. He felt weak, but wasn't in any pain. His left arm was bandaged, but after two days, he could sit up and talk sensibly, and he knew that he would be as right as ever in a week or two. The newspapers were yesterday's, and carried full reports of the raid at Wimbledon, but nothing about the fight at his flat. Alice was shown in every paper, but there wasn't a picture of Mae.

He was looking through this morning's paper, five minutes later, when the door opened and Loftus came in. Ross dropped the paper, and raised a hand in greeting. Loftus, walking slowly, came across and sat down on the foot of the bed, stretching his false leg straight out in front of him. They looked at each other for a few seconds, both grinning.

Then Loftus said: "Well, how's the hero?"

"Wonderful!"

"In future, you might remember that we like to keep our best agents alive," said Loftus. "You were crazy to go in like that—don't do it again." His grin broadened. "If you hadn't, we might have had more casualties and gone on for hours. And we might not have made Professor Conway so happy."

"How—how's his daughter?" asked Ross, as if casually.

"Doing all right. She wasn't hurt anything to speak of, and is tucked up in bed at home. Her aunt's fussing her, and her father looks about ten years younger. Job nicely completed, Peter."

"Some would say so. What did you find at the house?"

"Two dead men, one wounded, and two others who gave up when we rushed them. None of them was a big shot—it's all out, now. Higson of the Dive and Mae Harrison were the leaders, no doubt about that. We've found all the papers, all the evidence."

"Where's Mae?"

"Awaiting trial."

Ross didn't speak.

Loftus said gently: "And don't get any fool notion that you ought to have killed her, to save her from that. She asked for everything she's going to get. Sorry, Peter, but we needn't beat about the bush. What's more, the trial will do a lot of good, we'll be able to publish everything she's been up to, everything she's been doing. It'll tell the world that we've broken that particular gang, do something to make them realise British Intelligence isn't on its last legs yet."

"Ah," said Ross. "What was she doing, exactly?"

"Quite simply—running a small, highly organised spy-ring, selling whatever it collected to the highest bidder. Not always Russia, either. She's been at it for years. Elliott and Higson have talked freely, now she's caught. She's not insane within the legal meaning of the word, but obsessed with a hatred of England and all things English. I don't know her early history yet, but Higson says that all she ever worried about was harming the country. She did a lot during the

Second World War, and got away with it. Her background was so good that I couldn't find anything wrong with it, would have used her, within limits, to ease your personal troubles. You weren't the only one who was fooled."

Ross groped for cigarettes and lit one without thinking of offering the packet to Loftus.

"Two gangs were after Conway and the defence secrets—we don't know the other one, yet. We can guess! The first gang kidnapped Conway. Mae's mob—or rather Elliott—got in with them. For a while he worked for both, although he says he doesn't know much about the others, except that they were after Conway. He pretended to work for them, but was planning to get Conway from them, for Mae. He poisoned the men at the bungalow before they could get Conway away in the launch. Conway was drugged. Then he received the telephone message from the other bungalow. With Department Z men about he knew he would have trouble getting out, so he put on a policeman's outfit, kept at the bungalow, and slipped through the garden. He had the luck to pick up Alice."

"I see," said Ross. "This other gang——"

Loftus said: "Finding them will be our next job. Now! To bring the story up to date, there were underground offers of big money for these atomic air-defence plans, and Mae and Higson got to work on it. We soon found they were after Conway, whom they selected as the man to work on—because of his age and because of his daughter; they thought they could bribe her to help. You were keeping Conway pretty safe, and had been for months. Mae discovered it and made a set at you, and then—Higson isn't in any doubt—she fell in love. It complicated things somewhat."

Ross drew in the smoke, deeply.

"Mae wanted you out of the game, because she didn't want you hurt, and Elliott, your man with the Voice, simply acted on her orders.

"Mae kept ringing the changes, to confuse you, but you got on to Bray. She'd blackmailed Bray, who was mixed up in some gun-running during the First World War, but there were limits to what he would do—he'd found patriotism. So when you got warm, she switched suspicion on to Bray, and he certainly looked right. He'd done a great deal that she told him to.

"She was obsessed with you. She arranged for her own 'kidnapping', believing that if she were 'kidnapped', you'd be so desperately anxious to save her from further danger, you'd give up the case. Later, she let Bray give Elliott away. She also told Bray to let you think he'd had orders to start a quarrel—just another ruse to keep you thinking more about Mae than the case. She felt sure Elliott would get away from the Chancery Lane office, and had given Higson orders to kill him. A wounded man was a liability. She took the risk that you'd catch Elliott at Chancery Lane, of course—but she was so used to taking risks, it didn't worry her. Then she described him. That was very cunning, Peter, because she'd ordered him to wear the wig and false nose when Bray saw him—because she knew Bray would describe him, and if his description differed from hers, Bray would be on the spot."

Ross nodded, slowly.

"Tiger had been useful in some ways, such as supplying strong-arm men, and looking after Alice Conway, whom Elliott took to the garage, but he began to get ambitious. He was told to raid your flat first, then hers, to get you worrying about her. She hoped, even as early as that, that you'd give up if she were in danger. But Tiger was in danger himself. He looked for papers at her flat, and was obviously trying to muscle in. So Mae gave Tiger away—said just enough about the garage in the East End to make sure we'd go there. But she'd arranged for him and his wife to be killed so that they couldn't talk. You'd started to break Tiger, he wasn't loyal, and the only way to make sure he was safe was to kill him. She lost nothing there, but she put herself in the clear.

"By then you were so great a danger, and there was a risk you'd discover her real self, that she made an effort to kidnap you. Then she realised the game was pretty nearly up, but made her final effort with you. She still hoped the Wimbledon members of the group could get the plans. To confuse you, one of her men telephoned, pretending to be the Voice. Earlier, still wanting to find out exactly what you knew, whether you were on to Wimbledon or anything else, she offered help and did that little job with Bray and Dolly. She'd blackmailed Bray, of course, but he didn't know she was behind that. She was afraid there would be talk of a woman being concerned, and Alice Conway was nicely placed for a suspect—so she switched to her. Then gradually she realised that she couldn't win. She was afraid Higson or one of the others would break down, feared there'd be a raid at Wimbledon, and made that last attempt. She was nearly demented—and I don't have to tell you what followed."

Loftus stopped.

Ross stubbed out his cigarette, closed his eyes, and said quietly:

"Well, I don't want to run into anything like that again. Can't you invent a de-humanising serum, to make sure we don't make fools of ourselves?"

Loftus smiled.

"Forget it. Gordon's found out that if you stop a man from being human, you take something out of him that he needs on the job. The no-marriage rule wasn't vetoed just for the sake of it, it simply didn't work. Gordon hates to admit it, but that doesn't alter facts. Any questions?"

"Alice and Bray?"

"Oh, yes," said Loftus, "that was a curious little twist. Approach was made to Alice, through Bray—who was acting on his unknown blackmailer's orders. Alice was very curious, and wanted to find out who was so interested in her father's work. If she'd taken the normal course and gone to the police, she thought they would laugh at her. She saw herself as really doing something worthwhile—she'd led a drab life, and dreamed dreams. She knew her father was working on important projects, but didn't know what, and—well, she tried to find out just what Bray was after. He didn't really know her, had just tested her out and found she wasn't likely to fall for bribery. He knew what Conway was doing—Bray seems to know a lot that he shouldn't—and didn't like it. So he told his blackmailer that he couldn't get results, and dropped Alice. He had a strong motive, too—falling in love with his Dolly.

"Alice was kidnapped, as she told you, and fooled by Elliott, who was the 'policeman' you handed her over to. Since then, she's spent a lot of time telling herself that she was a fool, and promising she'd never complain about life being dull again."

Loftus smiled amiably.

Ross shrugged.

"Someone ought to do something about that," he said.

It was easy to find an excuse for visiting her; easy, after all, to show her that normal life needn't be dull. By the time the trial was over and the sentences carried out, Ross had come to look into a pair of startlingly blue eyes and know that they were his.

THE END

A Kind of Prisoner

John Creasey

Chapter 1
Homecoming

J udy Ryall heard the ring at the front door bell as she was moving from the kitchen to the sitting-room of the flat. She stopped in the tiny hall. The only light came from the sitting-room, but the door was nearly closed, and in the hall it was very dull.

It wasn't a long, steady ring; just brief and halfhearted, as if someone had touched the bell and then snatched a finger away.

Judy stood listening, her heart thumping.

Fear was an ugly thing; and by night it had become her constant companion. She could not fully understand it. It came whenever Alec was away. He was now, on another of his mysterious errands. She hated it. She hated his being away, but more than anything she hated the fear which crept upon her with the night's darkness. She knew of no reason for it; she tried to laugh at it, but could only hold it at bay during daylight. It always came on the wings of the dusk.

The bell did not ring again, but there was an unfamiliar sound; a panting sound. She could picture a dog, lying down after a long, exciting run; that was it, someone was panting.

Then she heard a different sound; the faintest ting at the bell, it could hardly be called a ring. Then came tapping, not sharp or hard, but muffled and slow. The panting came, also.

Then came a voice: "Judy," a man whispered, as if in pain: "Judy."

That was—Alec. Her husband; gasping the word.

Fright paralysed the muscles of Judy's mouth and her lips; and when she tried to move, her body seemed to resist. But she had to open the door now. She could just see the dark shape of the electric light switch. She stretched out a hand, and forced herself to go forward until she could touch it.

Light flooded the tiny hall, but brought no real relief, for at the same moment came another short, sharp ring at the bell; another hoarse: "Judy." She felt icily cold. She was close enough to open the door, now, but her muscles seemed dead. The panting noise continued, but the tapping had stopped and Alec didn't call out again.

She heard a thud, against the door.

"No!" she screamed, and with the cry there came some release from the paralysing fear. She slid the knob back and pulled the door wide, ready to scream again. But she did not.

Alec stood there.

Alec, her husband, Alec her lover and beloved, stood with the light shining on a face so pale that all the blood might have been drained from it. His eyes were huge, dark, filled with pain. He leaned against the side of the door, and his right hand was stretched out. He was gasping for breath; panting.

"Alec," she breathed, and there was no scream now, because of his desperate need. She took his arm, to draw him into the room. "Come in, and——"

He resisted her, and without being told, she knew that it was with a great effort. He licked his lips; he looked as if he might fall dead at her feet.

"Judy—ring this—number. Say you're my wife. Give the man——"

He stopped, but his lips kept working; it was as if the words he wanted wouldn't come. He stood with his huge pain-racked eyes and his desperately pale face, resisting his wife with one arm, and thrusting the other forward—with the envelope in it. It brushed against her hand.

"Give the man—who comes—this. Don't—don't open——"

He stopped again.

He turned his head—and sounds outside became clearer; footsteps.

Something happened to Alec. He thrust the envelope into Judy's hand, somehow compelling her fingers to close over it. Then he pushed her away. She couldn't resist, just staggered back. He did not look as if he had the strength, but there was no resisting his pressure.

"Lock, bolt, door." His voice suddenly became powerful. "Shut——"

He stretched forward, grabbed the door and closed it before she could move. It slammed. The bell gave a sharp ting. There were strange sounds outside, of movement and of voices. She shot the lower bolt, as a key scraped in the lock. The door shook but didn't open. Soon there came a long, urgent ring of the bell.

Alec had vanished; in his place was the solid wooden door, with the battery of the bell inside; and the bolts top and bottom.

Judy wanted to open the door, call Alec, help him, save him; but she did not. The bell rang again. She knew that there was desperation in Alec's mind, that although he might be dying, he was desperately anxious for her to do what he told her; he wanted that more than anything else in the world. She had known for a long time that he held his work more dear than life. Work—service. Mysterious, deadly, sinister secret service. This had begun the fear in her, vague at first until to-night; there was all the justification for fear.

All the horrors she had imagined had become real.

The bell jarred out again.

She put out a hand and shot the top bolt. She hardly knew what she was doing; she was not thinking beyond the words of his instructions, which she would never forget. She felt that they were the last words that he would ever speak to her, that obeying them was a trust.

She looked at the envelope.

It was just an ordinary cream-laid one, sealed, and with no address. At the top was scrawled a telephone number:

Whitehall 08181

Judy could hear that husky voice, hear words which had been uttered as if with the last effort he would ever be able to make.

"...ring this—number. Say you're my wife. Give the man—who comes—this. Don't—don't open——"

That was all, before the sounds had come from the stairs.

The bell rang again and there was a thud at the door; Judy knew that whoever was there would try to break it down. The light of the hall was bright upon her as she turned towards the living-room. Her mouth was dry, her face seemed stiff, her eyes were wide open, rounded, as if she couldn't close them. There was the warm, comfortable room, with the pictures which Alec had chosen and the precious things that they shared, and on the other side of the fireplace her chair, with the work-basket by its side, the light glinting on a pair of scissors.

The telephone was by Alec's big, winged chair.

"Ring this—number."

She looked down at it again, while the ringing at the door and the thudding stopped; and that seemed more ominous than the noise itself. *Whitehall* 08181. She actually lifted the receiver and began to dial, when a sound came at the window.

She screamed, dropped the telephone, turned. She gaped at the billowing curtains, at the man behind them and the open window. Fear worse than she had ever known held her in a vice. She could not move, could only stand with her mouth open, the telephone hanging from its platform, the letter in her hand.

The man jumped into the room, lithely; and landed as lightly and easily as a cat.

He smiled.

She had never seen him before. There was nothing remarkable about him; he was a little smaller than average, lean, youthful, hatless, wearing a brown coat. The thing which made him different was his smile. It wasn't at all sinister. At first it had no effect on Judy, except a negative one; it did nothing to worsen her fears. Then he turned his back on her, as the wind howled in. An ash-tray fell off a table, two photographs collapsed on the top of bookshelves on either side of the fireplace. As the window closed, calmness seemed to come into the room.

"Sorry to scare you, Mrs. Ryall," he said. He had a pleasant voice, and the remarkable thing was that his manner was so normal; somehow, he calmed her. "Sorry about it all. But we need your help." He smiled again, differently, as if trying to give her a message which words couldn't quite convey. "Alec would ask for it, too."

"Alec——" she began, and felt her body relaxing; it was almost as if the ice which had frozen in her veins was beginning to melt. "He——"

"I know, he's outside," the man said. "We'll do all we can. Did he give you this?" He moved towards her, but didn't take the letter. "And ask you to telephone Whitehall 08181?"

She found that she could answer. "Yes." His knowledge gave her confidence that this man was a friend of Alec. Afterwards she realised that there was no way of being sure, and that he might have fooled her; but at the moment she felt quite certain.

"May I?" He took it from her.

Another sharp ring came at the front door. It made Judy jump, brought fear back. But the man glanced calmly towards the door and didn't move.

"Impatient people," he said lightly. "They'll force it, soon. Mrs. Ryall, there's no time to explain, all I can say is that Alec would have wanted you to do this." He took another sealed envelope from his pocket—as the sounds grew louder outside. He ignored these, but scrawled the telephone number on this envelope, and handed it to her.

"Open the front door as soon as I've gone. Say this is what Alec gave you. Put up a fight." He kept smiling in that comforting way, although what comfort could anyone give her? "Make everything hard to get. We'll do all we possibly can to help Alec."

"Who—are you?"

"A colleague of Alec's," the man said. He was at the telephone, listening. "They've cut the wire. Better say you tried to ring the number on the envelope but couldn't get an answer. Will you?"

"I—I'll try, but——"

"I'll be seeing you," the man said. "Tuck that letter somewhere out of sight first." His eyes smiled. He stood by her side for a moment, gripping her wrist; his hand was strong, cool, steady. "Good luck, Mrs. Ryall. Fool 'em. Alec would want it."

He moved towards the window.

The scratching sounds were still audible at the front door.

The man pushed the window up, climbed out, then called almost in a whisper:

"Close it after me."

He stood up on the sill. This was the first floor, and there was a fall of thirty feet to concrete below; but he stretched up as if there were nothing at all to fear. He must have gripped something, for he pulled himself up. The curtains billowed in again, and all Judy could see were the man's legs; next his feet; then there was just the pitch darkness of the blustery night and the red curtain.

She closed the window, and turned round. She listened, but could no longer hear sounds at the door.

She had the second letter in her hand, stared at it, then moved suddenly and tucked it into the neck of her white blouse.

There were men outside whom Alec had wanted to outwit.

Her mind was hopelessly confused, but certain things made sense. Alec would want her to do what the unknown man had said; she had either to accept that or reject it, and she accepted it. She had to play for time; mustn't give the letter up at once. She had no idea who would come in, was simply certain that someone would.

She pulled back the bolts and the door opened.

Although she had been sure that it would, it set her heart beating wildly. Yet nothing in the appearance of the man who stood there need frighten. He was older than the one who had come in by the window, taller, rather gracious and almost benevolent looking. His hair was iron grey. He moved smoothly, and he smiled freely; but somehow there was no reassurance in his smile.

Another man was behind him.

"Stay there," this first man said to his companion and half closed the door before he approached Judy. She stood absolutely still, lips parted. "There's no need to be alarmed, Mrs. Ryall," the man went on. "Your husband will be all right—*if* you are helpful."

He smiled again and proffered cigarettes from a gold case—and intuitively, as she had trusted the other man, Judy felt savage hatred towards this one.

WANT ANOTHER PERFECT MYSTERY?
GET YOUR NEXT CLASSIC
CRIME STORY FOR FREE...

Sign up to our Crime Classics newsletter where you can discover new Golden Age crime, receive exclusive content and never-before published short stories, all for FREE.

From the beloved greats of the Golden Age to the forgotten gems, best-kept-secrets, and brand new discoveries, we're devoted to classic crime.

If you sign up today, you'll get:

1. A free novel from our Classic Crime collection.
2. Exclusive insights into classic novels and their authors and the chance to get copies in advance of publication, and
3. The chance to win exclusive prizes in regular competitions.

Interested? It takes less than a minute to sign up. You can get your novel and your first newsletter by signing up on our website www.crimeclassics.co.uk

CPSIA information can be obtained
at www.ICGtesting.com
Printed in the USA
LVHW09s0527260918
591388LV00001BB/238/P

9 781911 295853